THE SHATTERED

Book One of the Rift Cycle

By Alan Hawky

Table of Contents

Prologue

The night side of the world lay in a deep cobalt hush, a curved continent veined with city light, the pale seam of an ocean where waves chased the shore like silver moths. High above, where air thinned into cold glass, a ring of stations blinked in patient sequence, custodians of orbits and weather and the old promises of peace. The star at the center of the sky burned steady. The world turned. Nothing seemed to shake the long rhythm.

In the capital, the halls of governance were quiet. A floor of black stone reflected arches and lanterns and a ribbon of script that ran along the ceiling. The words were a vow that every child could recite by heart. This world was not alone. The worlds held each other. The bridges were sacred.

Far below those words, deep under the city, a chamber slept behind nine doors. The doors were plates of mineral grown in the planet's mantle, each tuned to a frequency that made teeth ache. The ninth door opened only when eight different hands, each bound by a separate lineage, turned eight separate keys. The chamber beyond was empty of ornament. It did not need ornament. It held the reason the bridges existed. It held the reason the bridges were ever needed.

No one called the thing inside an Engine in those days. There were other names, all of them ceremonial, any of them true. The device had grown where the planet grew. It had changed as the planet cooled. It reminded those who studied it of a seed that had learned to imitate metal. It reminded those who prayed to it of a heart.

It did not wake on its own.

A signal crossed the void, silent, perfect, a note that had waited centuries to be struck. It did not pass through wires. It did not ride a beam. It arrived everywhere at once. The stations felt it like a shiver passing through reinforced ribs. The bridges felt it as a pressure against their anchor pylons. In the chamber of nine doors, the device that was not a heart and not a machine rose on invisible currents and turned the way a listening face turns toward a song.

On a high balcony in the capital, an archivist watched the star. She had a small brass telescope and a ledger where she marked small, routine things. Meteors. Flight paths. Aurora forecasts. Her ink dried in the nib. The star brightened by a fraction no eye should have noticed. She noticed anyway, because it was her whole life to notice. Her breath misted the glass. She wrote nothing. There was no word for the feeling in her chest.

On a ferry that moved between towers, a boy in a red scarf pressed his palms to the window while his father pointed out ships in the harbor. The boy loved how the city rose from the crater lake like a dark flower. He loved the bridges, the ones in the sky more than the ones over water. He said he would build a new one someday, the longest one, the one that would never need repairs. His father smiled and nodded and said that would be a fine thing, and also a hard thing, and also a dangerous thing. The ferry hummed. The cable thrummed. The boy's scarf lifted in a draft and floated like a little flag of celebration.

The signal finished its transit or its bloom, and the chamber under the city became a bell. The walls did not vibrate. The air did not move. The people standing near did not hear it. But the planet heard. The continental plates remembered some very old order of alignment and tried to find it again. The ocean heard and rose to meet a moon that had not changed its face. The bridges heard. They pulsed with light from anchor to anchor, a fleet of veins in a body that had begun to clench.

In orbit, a ship that did not broadcast a name cut through the plane of the bridges at a angle meant to confuse the arrays. Its hull was a dark mirror. It took no light into itself. It shed no heat worth measuring. Inside, a single figure stood before a wall of translucent shells. Each shell held a sliver of what looked like stone and did not weigh like stone at all. The figure rested a hand on one particular shell. The sliver within glowed along a lattice no human hand had etched. The figure spoke to no one in particular. The words were not recorded. The meaning did not need language. It was a call to begin.

The device in the chamber answered.

Gravity, which is supposed to be the politest force, put away its manners. It gathered itself in the core and pulled with the focus of a mind. In the capital, glasses on dinner tables slid a finger's width and then returned. A mother steadied a vase and laughed and said it was only the train beneath the street. On the ferry tower, a cable gave one long drawn moan like a whale song sung backwards. The boy stared at the street below. The cobblestones curved. He blinked, and they were flat again. He told his father. His father said he had imagined it. He had not.

The star brightened again by that same small fraction, and again there should have been no eyes for it. In a monastery on a cliff over the southern sea, a young woman whose order learned to listen to stone set her palm against a piece of the mountain and felt the pulse of the world change. The beat became a stagger. Her bones rang. She fell forward and her forehead touched the rock and the rock whispered a word that made her bite through her own lip. She spat blood on the floor and whispered in turn to her teacher that the planet was afraid.

The teacher, who had a lifetime of patience carved into her face, did not say There is no such thing. She had felt it too. She reached for a bell cord and pulled. The rope was rough and real under her hand and she welcomed the pain as if it could anchor her in the old rhythm. The bell did not ring. The clapper struck and sound traveled, but distance had altered. The air near the ceiling was a separate sky. The sound wandered around the room like a blind bird and did not find the ears for which it was meant.

At the chamber of nine doors, the floors buckled. The doors bowed inward without breaking. The device turned again, as if following a map. It did not shine. It was more terrible than that. It drank. It took heat from hot things and made them luke warm. It took motion from moving things and gave it to still things. Water in pipes flowed uphill. A fountain became a perfect sphere above its basin and hung there like a captured moon.

Cracks appeared in the streets. Not the thin spiderwebs that come in summer and are sealed with tar. These were slim at the surface and opened wider as they descended, the mouths of creatures that live in darkness and have not eaten in a long time. The citizens of the capital saw the cracks and stepped over them and hurried to find their children. The archivist forsook her telescope and ran for the cabinet that held the glass plates where she stored the sky. She could save ten in her arms. She wanted to save a thousand. She had the sharpest thought of her life. She thought, The star is not brighter. We are more near.

The bridges howled. Their pylons were sunk deep into bedrock and into the bones of the broken moons and into tethered satellites that had been parked beyond the reach of storms. Those anchors held and then did not. The plasma that formed the body of a bridge does not like to be still. It is a highway made of hunger. It hunts along attractors and accepts the discipline of pylons because the pylons speak the language of the world. When the world changed its syntax, the bridges tried to learn the new grammar. They lengthened by a measure that made engineers clutch rails and blink and check instruments three times. They twisted. They sang a note that had killed pilots before. This time it carried more sorrow than anger.

In a village near the equator, a child alone on a field ran toward his house and felt the ground run faster than he did. The house slid closer like a toy pulled by a string. He reached the door and the door was not where he expected. He fell, caught the step with his shin, cried out, and the cry did not go into the air. It skated along the ground and into a storm drain and came up in the kitchen sink where his grandmother was washing a pot. The old woman wiped her hands and went to him at once. She did not scold him for dirtying his knees. She knew what the world felt like when it was about to change into something else. She had felt it once in her youth when a bridge had collapsed. This was a larger collapse. She felt it in her teeth.

In orbit, the ship with no name altered its vector and drifted along the limb of the planet the way a hunter paces the line of a forest. The figure inside watched the first city lights flicker and blink out, not one by one, but in patterns, as grid after grid went blind and then learned to see again. The figure touched another shell in the wall. The sliver within did not glow. It absorbed. It swelled with a darkness so pure it looked like a hole in the idea of vision. The figure gave a small nod, as though a lesson had been confirmed.

Somewhere under the eastern sea, the mantle tore.

The sound arrived everywhere. It had no respect for time. It was so low that the ear could not decide whether it was hearing or remembering. It came up through bed frames and window frames and piano frames. It made wine hum in bottles. It brought dust from rafters. In the capital, the archivist fell to her knees and her ledger slid from her hand and the ink jar toppled and the ink made a black river across the promise line on the floor.

The sea lifted and paused, held in the fist of the new gravity, then crashed in green walls that did not respect the borders inked on maps. Salt rushed into places that had not tasted it in a thousand years. In the monastery, the young woman who listened to stone crawled to the open door and saw the ocean at her own height and understood without language that the edge of the world was no longer where she had been taught to find it.

The device in the chamber bloomed. It did not flower. It unfolded axes. It reached through the planet along lines that geologists had inked in a hundred treatises, and along lines that no instrument had ever found. The planet fought back. It had a million levers and used them all. It liquefied rock in one place to absorb a shock from another. It gripped faults and held them like clenched fists. It spilled and drew back and spilled again. In doing so, it spoke. Not in words, not in any vocabulary the orders had cataloged, but in pressure and fatigue and a heat that cooled to grief. The listeners heard. Some fell asleep and did not wake. Some screamed until their voices tore. A few went very still and wept like children who have broken an old gift and cannot understand how their hands could do such a thing.

The bridges began to fail.

You could measure it. The pylons posted their warnings in dry diagnostics that ran red where they always ran green. You could feel it. The platforms at the midpoint ticked, ticked, ticked under loads they had never been asked to bear. Singers on the maintenance crews began to sing for real, not because the work called for it, but because their mothers had taught them to sing when doors wanted to stay closed and ladders wanted to throw you and engines wanted to keep their ghosts. Songs can hold a rhythm in place when the rhythm wants to go. The platforms ticked anyway. One by one, the midpoint stations let go of the old orbit, turned like beads on a broken necklace, and drifted into a new pattern that did not include safety.

On the ferry tower, the cable snapped with a sound that had no right to be so small. The gondola fell three meters and stopped, the emergency clamps biting clean and strong. The boy in the red scarf hit the window with his shoulder and dropped, stunned, into his father's arms. His father held him and took a breath that shook his whole body. They looked out together. The city had bent. Streets that once met at ninety degrees made a new angle. The lake in the crater was sloshing up and down as if it had been set upon a giant's knee. The father said his son's name. He said it again. The boy looked up and smiled the way children sometimes do when they are terrified and do not know the word for it. The scarf had slipped and hung outside the gondola like a tongue. It fluttered and then drifted upward toward the roof as gravity made a new suggestion.

Across the world, people did not run at first. They paused. And in that pause were ten thousand human things. A baker lifted a tray to save it, then put it down because it did not matter. A guard reached for a whistle and put his fingers against his lips and then stopped because the air had changed. A woman in a dark apartment unlocked the cabinet where she kept her mother's letters and reached to gather them, then stood with her hand on the paper as if paper could keep the world together. An old man put his hand on the table and closed his eyes and counted, not numbers, but days that had been kind to him, and thought that was enough.

Then they ran.

In the chamber, the device reached a threshold. If someone had been there with instruments that could read the language of thresholds, they would have written a number in a book and the number would have meant this. The thing can do more. The thing will do more. The thing does not know how to stop. That is what thresholds are for.

The mantle tore again, higher this time, nearer to human rooms. A new valley opened where no valley had been. A mountain that had never wanted to exist rose in the shallow water off a coast and blistered itself into an island while fishermen tried to row away from it and realized that the sea had become a hill and they were rowing uphill and their arms had become too small for hills and years and the last of their strength.

The planet cracked.

Not in one clean line. Nothing alive breaks that way. It began as a thousand hairlines, each thinking it might heal later, then each hearing the others and learning a new song and joining in. The lines met and learned to be a network. The network learned to be a boundary. The boundary learned to be a separation. Light leaked from places where no light should leak. The sky stopped being a single roof. It became a lantern with broken panes.

In orbit, the ship with no name turned again, a small correction. The figure inside, silhouetted against a map of spheres and shards that altered themselves as the model tried to keep up, rested both hands on the console and sighed. It was not regret. It was not pleasure. It was a tired sound, the sound of someone who had watched a thing happen too many times. When the first city split and the two halves slid past each other with an intimacy no architect had intended, the figure bowed its head as if in greeting.

The bridges that held began to hold in new ways. Some bent and caught drifting pieces of continent the way a fisherman catches a log that will crush his boat. Some snapped and became flails that knocked buildings from their foundations and then cooled and fell into the sea like sleeping serpents. Their lifeboats launched. Their sirens cut off because sirens cannot speak to you when there is only the sound of the planet. There were quiet places too. On a plateau far from any city, wildflowers shook their heads and seeds let go at the exact wrong time and will never know their mistake, and a hawk that had ridden the same thermal for seven years in spring found no thermal where it should have been and flapped twice and found a new one in a new place and kept its counsel.

The capital did not fall at once. The crater walls kept their grip. The city stayed whole as a body holds itself during a seizure, not out of strength, but out of memory. The archivist found herself on her feet without the moments between. She had saved five plates. They would not make a difference. She knew that, and she felt only relief that she had something to hold. The laboratory lights went through their sequence twice and died. Through the windows she saw fire in the streets where lamps had tipped and fuel had spilled. She saw a bridge tower lean the way a drunk leans before he makes a joke he will never finish.

The device in the chamber folded back into itself. It did not stop. It rested, the way a muscle rests between convulsions. The nine doors lay cracked but still set in their frames. The floor had become a series of terraces. The air was hot enough to blur straight lines. In that heat, something like a thought passed from the device into the stone. The stone carried it the way a rumor slips through a crowd. The thought traveled up into the streets and into the jagged spaces where streets had been and into the bodies of those who lay still and into the bodies of those who ran and into the trunk of a tree that had learned to lean toward a certain light and would have to learn a new light. It went into the ocean. It went into the sky. It set itself in the memory of the matter of the world.

In a hundred places across the system, other chambers woke. Some were emptier. Some were larger. Some were not chambers at all, but configurations of veins and crystals and pressure that had been waiting longer than the words for waiting. The signal reached them. They answered. The star went quiet for a breath and then came back with a color wrong enough to make a child cry. The ring of stations bent its orbit like a knee. The ship with no name slid into a shadow and became indistinguishable from the shadow.

The figure inside touched the console one last time. On the glass, a path resolved, thin as a hair, bright as a nail head in sunlight. The path led away from the ruin, across the tangle of new bridges that would be built, through regions that did not yet have names, toward a place that had been a secret so long that it had become a story and then a rumor and then an ache. The figure rested its forehead briefly against the glass and closed its eyes.

Far below, the world tore itself into Shards.

When the first of the great fragments found a new orbit, just stable enough to promise a future, the sound of it carried through rock and water and bone. The listeners would say later that the planet said one word. The word was not forgiveness. The word was not blame. It was a word that meant both. It was a word that said I am hurt and I am here.

On the high balcony, the archivist finally wrote a line. The ink shook. The letters wandered like children with lanterns on a festival night. She wrote, The sky is nearer. She wrote, The bridges will not hold. She wrote, We are becoming pieces of ourselves. Then she put down her pen and she went to find anyone she could help, because if the world was going to be made of fragments, then the smallest kindness suddenly mattered as much as the great engines under the earth.

In orbit, the nameless ship turned its dark face toward the next system where a similar device waited inside a different world. The figure watched the new path draw itself on the air, thin and bright, a seam that would be tugged and tugged again until the fabric learned to tear along it. The figure let out that tired breath once more and spoke softly into the quiet.

"The cycle begins again."

ACT I – Sparks in the Drift

Chapter 1 – The Smuggler's Run

The plasma bridge glowed like a wound across the void, a burning vein that stretched from one broken fragment of a planet to another. Freighters moved along its length, fat-bellied silhouettes trailing sparks from overloaded drives. The Bridge-Port at its midpoint was a hive of lights and shadows, where merchants, mercenaries, and thieves lived off the pulse of trade.

Kael Veyra's ship limped into the station's traffic lane on engines that rattled like old bones. He muttered a curse under his breath as warning lights flickered red across his console. His ship, the *Wraith's Fortune*, was little more than patched metal and stubborn wiring, but she always managed one more run.

The Meridian patrol craft that circled the port ignored him. Good. They were too busy scanning Forge-State freighters, shaking down Riftborn scrap-barges, and making sure the right bribes found the right hands. Kael angled his ship into dock and powered down with a sigh of relief.

Inside the docking bay, the air smelled of hot coolant, fried meat, and the ozone tang of discharged plasma coils. Crowds shuffled past: traders hauling crates of crystal dust, engineers arguing over repairs, and children weaving between legs with stolen wallets in their fists. Kael pulled his jacket tight, checked the pistol at his hip, and kept his head down.

His contact was waiting at the back of a market cantina, a Forge-State trader with the kind of face Kael never trusted. Too clean, too eager. The man gestured sharply for Kael to sit, then slapped a datapad onto the table.

"You're late," the trader said.

"I'm alive," Kael replied, leaning back in his chair. "That's better than most who run these lanes."

The trader sneered and tapped the pad. "Let's see it."

Kael slid the crate across the table. Inside, wrapped in a scrap of cloth, was a capsule the size of a fist. Its surface was black metal, etched with faint glowing lines that pulsed like veins.

The trader froze. His smile vanished.

"You didn't tell me this was Obsidian work." He pushed the crate back with trembling hands. "I won't touch it."

Kael frowned. "It's just a relic. Some rich collector—"

"Shut up." The trader stood quickly, eyes darting around the room. "You don't know what you're holding. No deal."

He left without another word, disappearing into the crowd.

Kael sat for a moment, staring at the capsule. His instincts told him to walk away too, to dump it in the nearest airlock and forget he ever saw it. But another part of him—the part that always dragged him into trouble—was curious.

He touched the capsule. The lines on its surface flared, and with a soft hum, a projection burst into the air above the table.

A starmap.

Not just any starmap. It showed the Shattered Belt itself: dozens of fragments in unstable orbit around a dim sun. And beyond, a faint pulse of light in the Drift. A place no map should mark.

Kael's chest tightened. This was worth more than any smuggler's haul. Maybe more than his life.

Then the alarms began to sound.

The cantina lights flickered, and shadows moved at the door. People scattered as figures in dark cloaks entered, masks polished like obsidian, eyes hidden behind mirrored glass. The Obsidian Order.

Kael cursed under his breath. He grabbed the capsule, shoved it into his jacket, and kicked over the table.

Blaster bolts cut the air. He dove, rolled, and fired back, shots searing the wall where the assassins had been an instant earlier. They moved too fast, too silent.

The market erupted in chaos. Vendors shouted, civilians screamed, alarms wailed. Kael sprinted through the crowd, weaving between stalls as the assassins pursued. He shoved aside crates of glowing crystal dust, knocking them into the air like sparks.

One assassin leapt onto a railing above him, staff-blade igniting with a hiss. Kael ducked, the weapon slicing past his head close enough to scorch his hair. He fired back wildly, buying himself a moment.

He burst into the docking bay, lungs burning. The *Wraith's Fortune* waited, battered and ugly, but she was home. Kael sprinted up the ramp, slammed the hatch shut, and hurled himself into the pilot's chair.

Engines roared to life. The ship shuddered as bolts struck the hull. He yanked the throttle, and the *Fortune* blasted free of the dock.

The Bridge-Port shrank behind him, its lights smeared across the void. In the viewport, the starmap projection flickered to life again, the faint pulse in the Drift glowing brighter.

Kael wiped sweat from his brow, heart pounding.

"What the hell did I just steal?" he whispered.

The capsule pulsed once, almost like it heard him.

Chapter 2 – The Priestess and the Shard

The Shard of Sanctum's Edge hung in a cracked orbit, a fragment of a world that had never quite healed. From the void, it looked like a crescent of stone lit by the weak glow of its dying sun. On its inner curve, cities clung to cliffs carved from ancient rock, their lights a constellation of their own. Beneath the surface, rivers of molten fire pulsed from the fractured core, rising in glowing vents that kept the people warm and the forges alive.

High above the cliff city of Aeylan, the wind sang. It carried dust that glittered faintly in the pale light and a whispering resonance that those with the gift could hear.

Liora knelt on a ledge at the edge of the cliff, her staff laid across her knees. Her robes stirred in the wind, plain gray with threads of silver at the hem. She closed her eyes and let her breath match the rhythm of the rock beneath her. Every Shard had a rhythm. If you listened closely enough, if you were quiet enough, it spoke back.

The staff vibrated faintly. A soft hum filled her bones. The cliffside whispered like an old friend telling a secret. At first the sound was like all the others she had known, echoes of memory, remnants of a world before the breaking. But then the tone shifted. It grew deeper. Urgent.

Liora's eyes snapped open. The vision struck without warning.

She saw darkness beneath fractured worlds, a vast machine like a heart of stone and iron turning slowly in silence. Around it, sparks of light like stars went out one by one. She heard voices not of her people, not even of humans, but something older, rising in unison.

The wounds stir. The sky will break again.

Her body convulsed. Blood filled her mouth. She gasped and the vision faded, leaving her trembling against the stone.

A hand gripped her shoulder. It was Elder Maelen, robed in white, his face lined with years of listening. His eyes were stern.

"You went too deep again," he said, steadying her. "The echoes are not meant to be followed so far."

"I heard them," Liora whispered. Her voice shook. "The Shards are changing. The voices do not only remember. They warn."

The elder's expression hardened. "Nonsense. The Shards sing eternal songs. They do not speak of futures. Only fools chase phantoms."

Liora clenched her staff, anger rising in her chest. "If we refuse to listen, if we blind ourselves, how will we ever know why the Shards broke? How will we stop them from breaking again?"

The elder turned away, his robes flaring in the wind. "Be grateful you still breathe. Another step down that path and your mind would have been lost to madness." He left her kneeling on the ledge, the reprimand echoing louder than the wind.

She stayed there long after he was gone, staring out at the fractured horizon. The glow of the core burned through cracks in the stone, a reminder that this world was alive, even in pain. She pressed her palm to the cliff. The resonance thrummed against her skin.

"Show me," she whispered. "Please. Show me what you need me to see."

The hum grew louder, not with words but with a direction. Her staff vibrated, pulling faintly toward the sky. Toward the Drift.

Her breath caught. She closed her eyes, and for an instant she saw him: a man running through fire and shadow, clutching a glowing map that pulsed with the same rhythm she felt now. She did not know his name, but she knew the Shards were binding them together.

That night, sleep came in fragments. Dreams burned in flashes: collapsing cities, fire raining from the heavens, a bridge torn apart by unseen hands. And always the man, faceless in shadow, clutching the map.

She woke before dawn, heart racing. She tightened her grip on her staff and whispered into the cold air.

"The Shards will call us together."

Chapter 3 – The Warden's Burden

The energy bridge looked calm from the command deck, a river of white fire that ran between two broken worlds. Patrol beacons strobed along its length in steady rhythm. Freighters moved like patient whales. The view made civilians believe in order.

High Warden Seris Thane knew better. Order lasted only as long as the people who enforced it.

She stood with her hands clasped behind her back, boots planted, gaze steady on the traffic lanes. The wardenship Resolve, a Meridian cutter with clean lines and a reputation that made smugglers mind their manners, sat in a slow drift beside the bridge. The ship's windows threw silver light across her uniform. The fabric was immaculate. The man inside it was not what mattered. The oath was.

Lieutenant Mara Pell approached with a slate and the look of someone who would rather be anywhere else. "Status sweep complete. No anomalies on the pylons. Tariff intake is on schedule. Customs flagged two Riftborn scrap-barges for inspection."

"Release the Riftborn with a warning," Seris said. "Their holds are empty. That clan always arrives empty and leaves full. Time the search for when they return."

Mara hesitated. "Command prefers visible enforcement."

"Then command can come do it themselves." Seris tilted her head toward the viewport. "We are here to keep the bridge open. Not to bully the poor."

Mara's mouth twitched. "Understood, High Warden."

A chime cut the air. The distress tone was sharp and unmistakable. Seris did not flinch, she only turned.

"Source," she said.

"Convoy freighter Laxmi, midspan, sector C," an ensign called from communications. "Under attack. Multiple small craft. Transponder masks."

Seris's voice sharpened. "Launch interceptors. All hands to alert. Bring us along the inner rail, slow. I want clean shots that will not clip the pylons."

Resolve slid from her idle drift and began to prowl. Two wardens, knife wing fighters with blue tails, peeled from their racks and kicked hard toward the midpoint. The bridge filled the view, a cathedral of plasma caged by pylons the size of towers. Beyond it, the night was full of shards and quiet fire.

"Patch me to Laxmi," Seris said.

Static hissed, then a voice, tight with fear. "Taking fire at cargo bay two. They know your patrol timing, Warden. They were waiting in the blind arc."

"They will not like what they caught," Seris said. "Hold your course if you can. Keep your ventral profile toward the pylons. It is thicker."

The fighters streaked into the convoy's shadow. On Seris's console, targets resolved, six raiders hugging the freighter's wake. Their signatures were muddy, heat bled into the bridge glare. Good pilots. Better planning.

"Wardens, lock and warn," Seris said. "If they turn toward the pylons, you break and do not follow. I would rather lose thieves than lose a bridge."

Green tags flashed to amber. The raiders scattered like startled birds. Two dove toward the rail and ran parallel to the pylons, trusting the no fire zones to shield them. The others threw chaff and vanished into the glare. A spray of blue fire licked across the freighter's flank. Armor peeled back like bark.

"Pursuit?" Seris asked.

"Negative," Mara said, eyes on her feed. "They knew when we would arrive, and when we would hesitate. They are gone."

Resolve drew alongside Laxmi. Fire crews in pressure suits poured foam across the rent hull. Med teams took wounded aboard. Seris watched in silence, jaw set. The pattern bothered her more than the damage.

She turned to Mara. "Pull the last twelve patrol schedules. Compare against convoy manifests. I want overlaps where our absences and high value cargoes coincide. Check who had access to both sets."

Mara blinked. "You think the schedules leaked."

"I think someone is selling roadmaps to murder. Work quietly. If I am wrong, we lose nothing. If I am right, I would like to learn it before the next convoy burns."

The lieutenant nodded and moved. Seris left the deck long enough to step into the med bay. The air smelled of antiseptic and hot metal. A cargo handler lay on a cot with a pressure bandage on his shoulder. Grease stained his fingers and cheek. He tried to sit when he saw her. She put a hand on his arm.

"At ease," she said. "You held your line."

He laughed once, then winced. "Only line I had, Warden."

"Lines are enough," she said. "You saved more than you know."

By the time she returned to the command deck, the council was calling.

The holo rose from the dais like a pale fountain and became faces, five of them, all silver pins and fine collars, all safe on a station that never smelled of burning insulation. Councilor Venn's mouth already held the shape of dismissal.

"High Warden Thane," Venn said, voice smooth. "We received your preliminary action report. Your response time was adequate. Losses are within acceptable thresholds."

"Acceptable to whom," Seris asked, calm as ice.

A different councilor, Prefect Hale, smiled without warmth. "You know the calculus, Thane. Trade requires risk. Our concern is that your patrols have become rather aggressive in the last quarter. Merchants complain. Our tariffs feel it."

Seris kept her hands still behind her back. "My patrols are not aggressive. Pirates are. The raiders knew our timing. They ran the blind sectors that exist for maintenance safety. They carry codes they should not have. Someone is selling them our maps."

Venn's eyes cooled further. "Those are serious claims."

"They are observations," Seris said. "I request a closed audit of schedule access, and a rotation of command codes for the next thirty days."

Hale waved a hand. "Denied. Shuffling codes creates friction. Friction slows trade. In any case, these incidents are episodic. In aggregate, traffic is up. Do not overreact."

Seris felt the old pulse of anger in her throat, then set it aside. "With respect, Prefect, traffic will cease to exist if a bridge falls. We stand on a knife's edge every day. You do not get to call that episodic."

"Mind your tone, Thane," Venn said. "You are valued, but you are not irreplaceable. Maintain order. Collect tariffs. The rest is politics for another room."

The holo dissolved. Silence filled the command deck like smoke.

Mara looked at Seris. The crew looked without looking. Seris exhaled and let the anger bleed into the air where it could not hurt anyone.

"Lieutenant," she said, voice even. "The audit proceeds anyway. Use only people you would trust with your life. If you hesitate on a name, do not use them."

Mara nodded once. "Yes, High Warden."

Resolve settled back to a holding pattern while repair crews finished on Laxmi. The bridge glowed, patient, a vein that pretended it could not be cut. On the far side of the viewport, a maintenance skiff drifted along the pylons. The workers inside sang as they went, a low call and response around the work lights. Seris listened for a heartbeat and let the sound lay a thin layer of calm over her thoughts.

When they docked at Anchor Spindle to file their reports and take on supplies, the station smelled like hot metal and old coffee. A banner on the concourse insisted that Meridian kept the peace. Below it, a cleaner was sweeping up broken glass with slow, careful strokes.

Seris walked the concourse alone, hands in her coat pockets, head bare. She preferred to be seen. It reminded people that Wardens were not only helmets and rules. She stopped at a stall for tea. The vendor's hands shook as he poured. He thanked her for being there, though she had done nothing visible. She thanked him back, because small courtesies held more weight than propaganda.

"Tired day, Warden," someone said behind her.

She did not turn at once. The voice was low, familiar from a hundred dockside deals and midnight confidences, the kind of tone that never belongs to anyone official. When she did turn, the man in front of her looked like every other stevedore on the station, broad shouldered, grease along his sleeve, cap pulled low.

"Kell," she said softly.

He ducked his head. "You remember a face too well."

"I remember debts," Seris said. "And favors. And whether a person keeps either."

Kell glanced past her at the crowd, then held out a wrapped ration bar. "For the road," he said, voice too loud now, the voice of a man talking about nothing. "A little extra sugar helps with the ship shakes."

Seris took it. The wrapper was heavier than a bar should be. She did not look down. She put it in her pocket and took a sip of tea.

"Watch your back, Warden," Kell said. "Not everyone here is who they claim."

"Are you," she asked.

"Today," he said, almost a smile, then vanished into the current of people.

Back on Resolve, Seris sat at her desk with the lights low and unwrapped the ration bar. The bar itself was real enough. Under it lay a chip, black and thin, sealed with tape.

She slotted it. The screen filled with manifests, all stamped with Meridian clearance. Agricultural equipment for outer shards. Medical supplies for Anchor Twelve. Crate numbers, seals, signatures. Overlayed in red were routing notes that did not belong, tiny course corrections that moved shipments through blind arcs and into the hands of couriers that never appeared in the official chain. The end points were Forge-State depots. The cargo designations did not match the masses. The mass was heavy metal and composite, not grain and gauze. Weapons, crated and laundered through the very authority meant to keep them out.

Seris leaned back and let the cold run through her. She had suspected. Seeing it in her hands was a different thing. She copied the data to an air-gapped slate and slid the chip into a burner case.

Mara buzzed at the door. "You asked for schedule overlaps."

"Come," Seris said.

The lieutenant entered with two slates. She looked tired in a way coffee cannot solve. "Three events where our patrol windows matched blind arcs and high value loads. The access list for both schedules is large. Too large."

"We will make it smaller," Seris said. She pushed one of the slates toward Mara, the one with sanitized excerpts. "This is what they are moving. Quietly. Through us."

Mara read, went still, and then met Seris's eyes. "How far up."

"High enough that if we say it aloud, we will be reassigned to count ore on a rock no one can name," Seris said. "So we will not say it. We will act. We tighten our own procedures. We randomize our patrols without filing the changes until after the fact. We keep the bridge open. We keep the people safe."

Mara nodded. "And the council."

"Will hear when there is no way to pretend not to," Seris said.

She stood, stepped to the viewport, and looked out at the bridge. The plasma river shifted in slow surges, light spilling across the hull. Somewhere along that glow, a family was walking a cargo spine with their lives on their backs. Somewhere, a captain was calculating margin against risk and lying to his crew about both. Somewhere, a pirate counted the seconds until the next blind arc and smiled because someone in a clean office had sold him the time.

Seris folded her arms, not to guard herself, but to keep from punching glass. Her reflection looked back, hard eyes, a streak of white at the temple she had not had last year.

"If the bridges fall," she said, quiet enough that only the room heard her, "it will not be pirates who break them. It will be us."

Chapter 4 – Ambush at Bridge-Port

The Bridge-Port of Halvek was a maze of steel and neon wedged into the midpoint of a plasma bridge. It hung between worlds like a tumor clinging to a vein, alive with commerce, corruption, and desperation. From orbit it looked fragile, a web of platforms and docking arms wrapped around the bright flow of the bridge. Inside, it was noise and stink and opportunity.

Kael Veyra moved through the markets with his collar turned up and his hand close to his pistol. The stolen capsule burned like a secret in his jacket pocket. His last buyer had run, terrified, and Kael needed another before the Order's shadows closed in.

Vendors shouted over one another, offering fragment-dust crystals, black-market ration packs, and knockoff Meridian rifles. The air reeked of hot oil and sweat. Kael's eyes flicked to every corner, measuring exits. His instincts screamed that the Order was already here.

He spotted a broker hunched over a table in a dim cantina carved into the hull. Kael slid into the seat across from him, pulled the capsule out just far enough for its faint glow to show.

The broker's face went pale. "You're mad," he hissed. "Put that away."

"You want it or not?" Kael asked.

The man pushed back from the table so fast his chair toppled. "No deal. Not with that." He bolted into the crowd, leaving Kael alone with the capsule.

Kael muttered a curse and shoved it back into his coat. He rose to leave. That was when the lights died.

The cantina plunged into darkness. For a heartbeat there was silence, as if the entire port was holding its breath. Then came the sound of boots, soft and synchronized.

They emerged from the shadows like wraiths. Tall figures in black cloaks, faces hidden behind mirrored masks that caught the faint neon glow. The Obsidian Order.

Kael's gut clenched. He drew his pistol as the first assassin moved.

Blaster fire ripped through the room. Patrons screamed and dove for cover. Kael ducked behind a table, returned fire, and sprinted for the door. The assassins moved with eerie precision, silent even as they struck. One vaulted onto a railing, a shard-blade hissing to life in their hand.

Kael dove as the blade slashed where his head had been. He scrambled into the market, shoving through panicked civilians. His heart pounded. The capsule felt heavier with every step.

The assassins followed without sound, their mirrored masks reflecting the chaos.

Kael's lungs burned. He turned a corner into a maintenance corridor and nearly collided with a young woman.

She stood calm amid the chaos, staff across her palms, eyes luminous in the dim light. Her robes marked her as an Echo Priestess.

"Out of the way," Kael snapped, pushing past.

The assassins rounded the corner behind him. The woman lifted her staff and struck it against the floor.

The air vibrated. The walls themselves seemed to hum. A wave of resonance rolled through the corridor, making the assassins falter as if the Shard itself had spoken against them.

Kael froze, staring. The woman's face was serene, but her eyes burned with purpose.

"Come with me," she said.

"No chance," Kael shot back, raising his pistol. "I don't need—"

A shard-blade hissed past his cheek, cutting into the wall. Kael stumbled back. The priestess grabbed his arm, her grip surprisingly strong.

"If you want to live," she said, voice steady, "you need me."

Kael's mind raced. He hated zealots. He hated priests. But he hated dying more.

"Fine," he growled. "But you're paying for the repairs if my ship gets wrecked."

Together they ran, weaving through maintenance shafts as assassins closed in. The priestess struck her staff against the walls, sending pulses that shook loose pipes and dropped panels in the assassins' path. Kael fired blindly over his shoulder, buying seconds at a time.

They burst into Dock Nine, where the *Wraith's Fortune* waited in its berth, scarred and patched but alive.

Kael sprinted up the ramp, dragging the priestess behind him. Blaster fire scorched the bulkheads. An assassin vaulted onto the ramp, blade flashing. Kael kicked the release and the ramp shuddered upward, crushing the figure between metal plates. The scream that followed was muffled but chilling.

Kael threw himself into the pilot's chair. The priestess steadied him with one hand as he fumbled with the controls. Engines coughed, then roared. The *Fortune* ripped free of the dock, alarms howling behind them.

Through the viewport, the plasma bridge arced like lightning across the void. Behind them, the Order's ships detached from the port, pursuit lights flaring.

Kael slammed the throttle forward. "Who the hell are you?"

The woman met his gaze, calm even as the ship rattled under fire. "My name is Liora. And I was sent to find you."

Kael cursed under his breath. He did not believe in fate, but the look in her eyes unsettled him more than the assassins.

The capsule pulsed in his pocket, its glow seeping through the fabric. The map projection flickered in the cockpit, pointing deeper into the Drift.

Kael's grip tightened on the controls. He had the feeling his life had just been stolen out of his hands.

Chapter 5 – Unlikely Allies

The *Wraith's Fortune* limped away from Halvek with scorch marks along her flanks and a trembling in her ribs that Kael felt through the pilot's chair. Warning glyphs winked along the console like a rash. One engine ran hot. The other sulked. The hull integrity readout suggested optimism that the metal did not share.

Liora sat in the co-pilot seat with her staff across her knees. She had closed her eyes, as if the chaos of the escape had never happened. The faint crystal in the head of her staff thrummed, so soft that Kael almost doubted he heard it at all. The cockpit smelled of hot wiring and the sweet copper of singed insulation.

He flicked switches and rerouted power with practised hands. "You picked a fine time to show up, Priestess."

"Liora," she said, calm as a held breath. "And I did not pick the time."

"Right. The universe did. Or a rock whispered a schedule."

"The Shard called," she said. "I followed."

Kael snorted. "Well, tell it thanks. Next time it can send a repair crew."

Out the viewport the bridge dwindled to a bright thread, then to a memory. Beyond it the stars were crowded by dark stone. A field of debris drifted there, slow and treacherous, the afterbirth of a thousand small collisions. The ship's proximity alarm gave a half-hearted bleat.

Liora opened her eyes. "We are not safe yet."

"You noticed." Kael tapped a control and brought up a scatter of pale dots. "Magnetized slag, old hull plates, bits of rail. The station dumps its trash this way. The field is shallow, but it plays havoc with guidance. Hold on."

He slid the *Fortune* into the first channel. A shard of black metal spun past, close enough to leave a bright scratch on the portside viewport. The ship shivered. Relative velocity spiked and fell. The stars wobbled.

"Your ship is anxious," Liora said softly.

"She is honest." Kael kept his eyes on the scope. "Honest ships complain before they break."

A heavier tone rolled through the hull. The magnetometer spiked. The field was changing as they moved, a messy turbulence like weather without sky. Kael narrowed his eyes. "That is not right."

"The Drift remembers," Liora said. She put her palm against the bulkhead, as if feeling a pulse. "Some of this metal came from Shards. It still holds their song."

"They are scrap," Kael said. "Scrap does not sing." Another spike. The channel he had chosen began to close like a throat.

Liora stood. "You will not like this."

"Start with that, why do not you."

She stepped behind his chair, reached past him, and planted the staff against the floor where two struts met. The crystal hummed. The hum rose until the edges of the cockpit softened, as if distance itself had become a little uncertain. Panels vibrated. Loose screws chattered in their seats.

"Enough," Kael snapped. "You rattle this crate any harder and she will come apart."

"Trust me." Liora kept her voice even. "The debris is not still. It is coasting along a pattern you cannot see. I can feel the gaps where that pattern is thinnest. Feather the starboard thruster. Ease down three degrees. Now, short pulse. Now, wait."

He almost refused on reflex. Pride and habit made his mouth tight. Then the hull wailed as a plate the size of a door slid past their bow. He swallowed a curse and did as she said, gentle nudges that felt wrong to a pilot who loved decisive motion. The ship crept. The alarm quieted. A curl of iron dust whirled in eddies outside and did not touch them.

They fell through a narrow pocket where the drag vanished. Kael let out a breath he had not known he was holding. "Luck."

"No," Liora said, quiet but firm. "Resonance."

He risked a glance at her. She had sweat at her temples, fine as mist. The hum of the staff eased to a purr. He kept his hands light on the controls and let her voice carry the rhythm of their path. Short pulse. Wait. Drift. Now. They threaded the last of the field and came out into a small clean dark that felt like open water after breakers.

Kael cut the throttle and set the ship to a lazy spin while the engines cooled. He pinched the bridge of his nose. "I do not believe in your voices. But I am not arguing with results."

"I am not here to make you believe," she said. "I am here because the Shards do not want to break again."

The cockpit lights steadied. Kael stood, the adrenaline finally leaking away, and felt the ache in his shoulders. A shallow cut burned along his forearm where a flying panel had kissed him in the scramble. He reached for a rag.

"Let me," Liora said.

"I have had worse."

She wrapped a strip of cloth around his arm with practised hands, quick and neat. "It will sting less if it is clean."

He watched her for a beat. "You patch people up between sermons."

"We rarely preach," she said. "We listen. We help. We move on."

"Sounds lonely."

"It is." She tied the cloth and met his eyes. "Your life sounds noisy. That is also lonely."

He made a noncommittal sound and sat again. The capsule weighed at his chest. He pulled it free. The black metal drank the dim light. A faint pulse moved along its etched lines.

"Do you know what this is," he asked.

"I know what it points to." Liora reached out. "May I touch it."

He hesitated. "Try anything and I vent it out the airlock."

She nodded and laid her fingers on the capsule. The change was instant. The map sprang into being above the console, but where before it had been a feverish flicker, it now steadied and brightened. The Shattered Belt resolved in clean arcs, each fragment a gemstone lit from within. A thread of light laced away from the bridge lanes, out toward the Drift. The thread had more detail now. It split and rejoined the way a river does when it meets a low island. Along its length, tiny glyphs pulsed like heartbeat markers.

Kael swore softly. "It likes you."

"It responds to resonance." Liora studied the path, eyes moving. "It wants a listener who can match its tone."

He reached up and rotated the projection. The glyphs slid with his hand. He stopped over a cluster that did not match any charts he owned. "I know this sector. Or I thought I did. There is nothing here."

"There is," Liora said. "It was empty. Now it is not. The pattern changed."

He closed the capsule in his palm. The map died. For a heartbeat the cockpit felt colder.

"So," he said. "You, a stranger with a stick, walk onto my ship and tell me that the map is singing. That is very nice. Here are my rules. You do not touch my navigation without asking. You do not pray over my engines. You do not invite more assassins aboard."

"You have my word," she said.

"And the map is not for sale until I say so."

Liora's gaze hardened. "That is my rule. You will not sell it at all. Not to Meridian. Not to the Forge-States. Not to anyone who will turn it into a tool for power."

He laughed, sudden and sharp. "I am a smuggler. I sell things. That is the one part of my life that makes sense."

"It will kill people if you sell it."

"Everything kills someone," he said. "Tariffs do. Bridges do, when they fail. Good intentions do when fools build plans on them."

"It will kill whole Shards," she said, and there was no tremor in her voice. "And you know I am not speaking in riddles."

Silence held for three breaths. The engines ticked as they cooled. Kael stared at the dead capsule and saw not credits, but fire raining through the sky of the place he had been born. He swallowed against a dry throat.

"Fine," he said. "I do not sell it. Not yet. We find out what it is. Then we talk."

She exhaled, a small sound that might have been relief. "Then we have an agreement."

He tucked the capsule away. "It lasts until you start chanting and my ship starts floating sideways."

A faint smile touched her mouth. "I will warn you before I sing to your bulkheads."

Kael leaned back. The worst of the tremor had gone from the *Fortune's* bones. Outside, the Drift stretched like an empty road at night. He keyed the passive scanners. A scatter of pings returned. Merchant lanes. Old beacons. A Meridian probe. Then a new ping, narrow and cold, from behind.

He did not have to say the name. Liora glanced at the scope and nodded. "The Order."

"They are good at following," Kael said. He killed the spin and brought the engines up in a low whisper that would be harder to catch. "Better than I am at being followed."

"You used to run with the Riftborn," she said. Not a question.

He did not answer at once. He watched the numbers creep. He felt the old bitterness try to rise and parked it. "For a while."

"You left."

"I broke a deal. People paid for it." He rubbed his thumb over a nick in the throttle. "You get tired of seeing your own choices come back with knives. You either change trades or change yourself."

"And you changed trades."

He smiled without humor. "I am choosing. Slowly."

Another ping. Closer. The *Fortune* groaned as he asked for more speed. The hot engine complained. He coaxed it with small adjustments, nothing harsh, the way you calm a horse that remembers a fall.

Liora studied the dim path only she could see. "I can keep masking our signature for a little while. Not long. They know how to listen too."

"Then we stop making straight lines," Kael said. He set a course that bent along weak gravity contours, a crooked path that made no tactical sense to an impatient hunter. "And we learn what this map is worth, truth first, credits later."

Liora rested her staff across her knees again. "There is a place where the path thins. A hollow Shard, dead for a very long time. The old stones there hum like a hive."

He glanced at her. "You saw it."

"I heard it."

He nodded once. The ship's nose tilted toward an emptier part of the sky. "All right, Listener. We will go where your hum says. You help me keep us ahead of the masks. I will keep this crate in one piece."

She settled into the co-pilot chair and fastened the straps with quick, certain hands. "You do not like priests," she said, almost curious.

"I do not like anyone who thinks their answers are the only ones," he said. "I especially do not like anyone who comes aboard and starts making rules."

"You made rules first."

He found himself smiling despite the tightness in his chest. "Fair."

They moved together through the next set of checks with an ease that surprised him, his practical motions and her quiet listening dovetailing more cleanly than he would ever admit. The pursuit ping faded, then returned, then faded again. It would not quit. That was fine. Nothing worth keeping ever came without something chasing it.

The map's dead weight warmed against his chest. Out beyond the scopes, a thin route waited, bright for those who could hear it, invisible to the rest. Kael set the course and felt the ship lean into it.

"Looks like you are a passenger for a while," he said.

Liora shook her head. "No. A partner."

He did not argue. The *Wraith's Fortune* slid into the dark, small and stubborn, a flick of light moving toward a place the charts refused to name. Behind them, in the cold black, a narrow signature kept pace, patient as a shadow. Ahead, the Drift deepened, and somewhere inside it, old stone began to hum.

Chapter 6 – Council's Rot

The Meridian capital station was built like a crown. Its tiers rose around the axis of a great spindle, polished metal and glass catching the pale glow of the system's star. Trade ships docked in neat lines. Banner holograms pulsed with the Accord's crest, a silver circle crossed with clean cracks. To outsiders it projected order and stability. To those who lived inside its walls, the cracks were deeper than the symbol admitted.

High Warden Seris Thane stood in the council chamber with her hands clasped tight behind her back. She kept her shoulders straight, her jaw set, her eyes cool. Across from her, five councilors sat in a half circle, their robes trimmed with silver thread, their expressions polished smooth as stone.

The chamber was cavernous, ringed by tall windows that framed the plasma bridge outside. It was meant to remind everyone who entered that Meridian controlled the arteries of the Shards. Seris saw it only as a cage.

Councilor Venn spoke first. His voice had the clipped edge of someone used to obedience. "Your patrol report was received. Another pirate strike, another distress call. Yet the numbers remain consistent with projections. This is not crisis. It is commerce."

Seris kept her voice level. "The convoy was targeted with precision. The raiders knew exactly when and where our patrol would leave a blind arc. That is no coincidence. Schedules are leaking."

Councilor Hale lifted a jeweled hand. "Unproven. Your report cites circumstantial alignment. Pirates have always been resourceful."

"They had our codes," Seris said. She felt her control strain, but she kept her tone cool. "The kind that should cycle every week. They did not guess. They were given."

A murmur passed between the councilors. They did not deny it, but neither did they admit it.

Councilor Sira leaned forward. She was younger than the rest, her eyes sharp, her smile sharper. "You are implying corruption within the Accord itself. Be careful, Warden. Accusations without evidence border on insubordination."

Seris's hands tightened behind her back. She thought of the data chip hidden in her quarters, the manifests Kell had risked his life to give her. Weapons routed through official corridors, sealed with Meridian signatures. She wanted to slam the evidence on their table and watch their masks crack. But that would burn her last card too soon.

"I am not implying," Seris said evenly. "I am observing. The bridge will not care for our politics when it falls. Nor will the dead. I recommend an immediate audit of schedule access and cargo routing. Quietly, before another convoy burns."

Councilor Venn's eyes were cold. "Recommendation denied. We cannot afford the disruption. Order requires consistency. Commerce requires trust. If we begin chasing shadows, we project weakness."

"Order requires truth," Seris said.

Silence pressed the chamber. Four of the councilors stared back with expressionless faces. Only Sira's smile widened, like a predator scenting blood.

Venn tapped the table. "Enough. You are a soldier, not a strategist. Follow your orders. Maintain the bridges. Collect tariffs. Leave politics to those who understand them."

The dismissal stung more than the words. Seris bowed stiffly and left the chamber before her temper snapped her oath in half.

The corridors outside were full of petitioners and clerks. The air smelled of incense and machine oil. She walked quickly, ignoring the eyes that followed her uniform. Her boots rang against polished stone.

Mara Pell was waiting in her quarters when she returned, slate in hand, her face pale. She had pulled her hair back in a rough knot, no time for discipline.

"You were right," Mara said quietly, as soon as the door sealed. She set the slate on the desk. "Three overlaps in the last two months. Convoys routed through blind arcs, patrols shifted at the last minute. All signed off by senior council staff."

Seris picked up the slate. The numbers stared back, cold and damning. "So it is true."

Mara swallowed. "If we push this, we will not just be reassigned. We will disappear."

Seris set the slate down with deliberate care. "Then we push carefully. Rotate codes ourselves. Randomize patrols without warning. Report it late, not before. If we cannot clean the council, we can at least keep the bridges alive."

Mara nodded, relief flickering across her tired face. "And the proof?"

Seris thought of Kell, the ration bar, the chip. She thought of the manifests, the weapons bound for Forge-State depots. The proof was poison. She would need to choose the moment to use it carefully.

"Not yet," she said. "When it cannot be ignored. Not before."

She stepped to the viewport. The bridge outside burned like a frozen river of light, steady, patient, fragile. Her reflection stared back at her, lined with shadows she had not noticed before.

"If the Accord has rotted," she murmured, "then someone must hold the spine straight. For as long as it will bear."

Her voice was low, but the words rang inside her chest with the weight of a vow.

Chapter 7 – The Warlord's Desire

The Forge-State of Varak rose from the scar of a broken world. Its cities were carved into cliffs of black basalt, its furnaces fed by the heat that bled from the planet's cracked heart. Smoke plumes curled into the thin sky. Great chains anchored floating platforms above the vents, each carrying smelters that roared night and day. To outsiders it was a vision of hell. To those who lived within, it was strength made visible.

At the highest point of the fortress city stood the Hall of Iron, a citadel hammered together from ship hulls and stone, its walls dark with soot and its windows glowing with the orange light of the foundries below. Soldiers drilled in the yard with exo-armor suits that made them towering silhouettes. Their boots struck the ground in unison, metal echoing across the cliffs.

Drax Korren watched from a balcony. His mechanical arm rested on the railing, the fingers flexing with a faint whine of servos. His real hand, scarred and heavy, held a goblet of molten steel that had already begun to cool. He drank it as if it were wine, letting the heat sear his throat. He did not flinch.

A captain in burnished armor approached and bowed. "Warlord, the raiding fleets return. They bring spoils, and prisoners."

Drax did not look at him. "I did not ask for prisoners."

"They believed information might be useful."

"Belief is weakness. Facts are useful." Drax turned at last, his dark eyes hard as forged iron. "Bring me the one who claims to know something worth hearing."

The captain nodded and left. Moments later, two soldiers dragged a figure into the hall. The prisoner was thin, clothes torn, one eye swollen shut. He stumbled as they shoved him forward. In his trembling hands, he clutched a satchel.

"This one begged to see you," a soldier said.

Drax descended from the balcony. His steps were deliberate, heavy. The prisoner flinched when the warlord stopped before him.

"You claim knowledge," Drax said. His voice was deep, a voice that filled the chamber without rising. "Speak."

The prisoner swallowed. "A relic, my lord. Smuggled from Meridian space. A capsule. It carries a map—"

Drax's hand shot out. He seized the man by the throat and lifted him as though he weighed nothing. "Do not toy with me. There are a thousand maps in the Belt. A thousand lies whispered by priests and smugglers."

"This is different," the man gasped. "It glowed. It showed… a path. Into the Drift. The Order hunts it. They say it leads to… to the First Shard."

The hall went silent. Even the soldiers stiffened. The term was forbidden, whispered only in myths.

Drax's grip tightened. "The First Shard," he repeated, his voice low and dangerous. "You saw this yourself."

The prisoner's face turned red, his eyes bulging. He could not speak, only nod frantically.

Drax released him. The man crumpled to the floor, clutching his throat. Drax turned to his captains.

"Prepare the fleets," he said. "Double the forges. Sharpen every blade. If this relic exists, it is mine. The Order hunts it because they fear what it awakens. Meridian hides it because they fear who will use it. But I…" He spread his arms, mechanical and flesh, towering over them. "…I will wield it. And when I do, the Shards will no longer drift like beggars around a dying sun. They will kneel. One Belt. One law. One will."

The captains slammed fists to their chests. A chant rose, harsh and rhythmic, echoing through the hall.

Drax Korren smiled, and it was a terrible thing. "Send word. Every smuggler, every clan, every spy. Bring me the thief who holds the capsule. Alive if possible. Dead if necessary. The map is all that matters."

He lifted his goblet again, the steel now hardened to a dull block. He crushed it in his hand. Shards of metal fell at his feet.

"The sky broke once," he said, his voice carrying like a hammer strike. "I will break it again. This time, into order."

Chapter 8 – The Silent Assassin

The halls of the Obsidian Order were carved from stone older than the Shattering. They lay hidden deep inside a hollow fragment, its surface black as glass, its interior veined with crystal. Torches burned low along the walls, though the fire was unnecessary. The crystals glowed faintly with their own light, pulsing in rhythms no two ever shared.

The assassin moved silently through the corridors. Cloak brushing stone, mirrored mask reflecting the glow, they seemed less a figure than a shadow wearing a body. No sound betrayed them, not even the shift of breath.

At the heart of the hall stood the Chamber of Glass, a circle lined with tall panes of polished obsidian. Reflections shimmered across the surfaces, dozens of masked faces looking back where only one stood. The Elder waited in the center, draped in robes darker than the void outside.

"The capsule has surfaced," the Elder said. Their voice was soft but cut like a shard of glass. "It carries the path. The Meridian do not understand it. The Forge-States will try to take it by force. But we, we who listen deeper, know what it awakens."

The assassin bowed their head. Words were unnecessary. Their silence was itself a vow.

The Elder circled them slowly, robe brushing the floor. "You were once a listener too. You heard the Shards and found only lies. That disappointment has made you sharper. You know the voices twist. That is why you sever them."

The assassin's fingers flexed, brushing the hilt of the shard-blade at their hip. A faint tremor passed through their mask, not emotion, but memory.

"Find the smuggler," the Elder continued. "He carries the relic. A priestess travels with him. An Echo. She will resist you. She will believe she hears truth."

The assassin finally spoke, voice a rasp like stone on stone. "The Shards do not sing. They scream. I will silence her."

The Elder inclined their head. "Do so. But remember—the capsule must be taken intact. If it awakens further without us, it may draw the Engines. And if the Engines stir uncontrolled…"

They did not finish the sentence. They did not need to. The crystals in the walls pulsed once, dimmed, and then went dark, as though the fragment itself shivered at the thought.

The assassin turned to leave. Their steps made no sound.

Before they vanished into the corridor, the Elder called once more. "Do you fear failure?"

The assassin paused. The mask tilted slightly, reflecting a dozen ghostly selves in the chamber's obsidian mirrors.

"No," they said. "I fear memory."

And then they were gone, swallowed by the shadows that had birthed them.

Chapter 9 – Flight into the Drift

The *Wraith's Fortune* groaned like an old beast under strain. Kael had coaxed worse ships through worse storms, but even he knew the Fortune wasn't made for what lay ahead. The console lights blinked in sickly yellow, warning him of everything from overheating coils to stress fractures in the hull.

Out the viewport, the stars were vanishing. One by one, they drowned in a spreading haze of dark stone and frozen wreckage. The Drift.

Kael spat into a rag and wiped sweat from his temple. He hated the Drift. No pilot trusted it. Gravity buckled in strange places, light bent, time itself seemed to stretch or tighten without warning. Ships went in and didn't come out. And now, thanks to the glowing relic in his pocket and the stubborn priestess in his co-pilot seat, he was about to take the Fortune straight through its throat.

"You don't have to look so grim," Liora said softly.

She sat perfectly still, her staff resting across her knees, robes neat even in the rattling cockpit. Her eyes were half-closed, as if she were listening to something Kael couldn't hear.

"I always look grim when flying into a graveyard," Kael muttered. He adjusted the throttle, easing them closer to the debris field. "You realize this is suicide, right?"

Her lips curved into the faintest smile. "If it were suicide, the Shards would not call us here."

"Shards don't call anyone." Kael smacked the console when the port thruster stuttered. "People make choices. Bad ones. This is one of mine."

A sharp ping cut through the cockpit. Pursuit. Kael cursed under his breath.

He brought up the scope. Behind them, three cold signatures flickered at the edge of sensor range. Too faint for Meridian patrols. Too precise for pirates.

"The Order," he said.

Liora opened her eyes. They glowed faintly in the dim light. "They are patient hunters."

"They'll have to be faster than me," Kael said. He gripped the throttle, leaned forward, and whispered to his ship like he always did in moments like this. "Come on, girl. Just a little further."

The *Fortune* dipped into the Drift.

Instantly, the world changed.

The stars smeared into streaks. The debris wasn't drifting lazily, it was alive, whirling in impossible eddies as though caught in invisible currents. Hull plates spun end over end. Broken engines tumbled like dice. Frozen bodies turned slowly, their eyes empty sockets staring through shattered visors.

The Fortune's alarms screamed. Kael swore and yanked the controls, weaving between jagged shards of metal. His hands were fast, but his eyes kept losing track. Distances lied. Objects seemed far, then slammed close. Others loomed huge, only to vanish like smoke.

"Easy," Liora said. She reached out and touched the console, her staff vibrating faintly. The hum traveled into the ship's frame, settling the vibration of its bones. "Listen."

"I am listening. All I hear is the hull tearing apart."

"No." Her voice was calm, steady. "Listen deeper."

Kael gritted his teeth but slowed his breathing. The ship groaned around him, yes, but underneath was a different sound. A rhythm. A kind of slow, sorrowful pulse, like a heart that refused to stop beating even as it bled.

He shivered.

"The Shards remember," Liora whispered. "They remember being whole. They remember breaking. And they are afraid."

Kael wanted to snap at her, tell her he didn't believe in haunted rocks. But something in that pulse dug under his skin. He tightened his grip on the controls instead.

The scope flared. The Order's ships were closer now, slipping into the Drift behind them. Their silhouettes were angular, predatory, engines glowing faint blue. They didn't falter at the debris. They moved as if the wreckage parted for them.

Kael's blood ran cold. "They're not even dodging."

"They know the paths," Liora said. Her voice had hardened now, stripped of calm. "We must go deeper."

Kael shot her a look. "Deeper? Lady, we're already one breath away from being paste."

"The capsule guides us. Trust it."

"I don't trust anything that glows in my pocket."

The ship shook as a chunk of shattered station spun past, clipping the outer hull. The lights flickered.

Kael swore. "Fine. Show me where, then!"

Liora closed her eyes. The capsule pulsed brighter in Kael's jacket. The starmap flickered into life in the cockpit, lines of light threading through the chaos. Where Kael saw only wreckage, the map showed channels, narrow but real.

"This way," Liora said. She pointed.

Kael followed, teeth clenched, sweat running down his neck. The Fortune dove between two tumbling towers of steel. A wrecked cruiser spun slowly above, its hull cracked open like a ribcage. Kael threaded the ship through a gap so tight the paint scraped off.

The Order's hunters followed, precise and unhurried.

"Damn it, they're gaining," Kael growled.

"They will not stop," Liora said. "But neither will we."

Ahead, the map's glow pointed to a hollow fragment. A dead Shard. Its core was split, leaving a cavern big enough to swallow ships whole.

Kael's instincts screamed no. Everything about that cavern promised death. But the map pulsed harder. Liora's eyes glowed faintly.

"That's insane," Kael hissed.

"It is the path," she said.

Behind them, the Order's ships opened fire. Blue lances seared past, clipping debris, turning chunks of stone into dust.

Kael slammed the throttle forward. The Fortune lurched, her engines shrieking. The cavern loomed ahead like the open mouth of a beast.

"Hold together," Kael whispered to his ship.

The Fortune dove into the dark.

The cavern swallowed them whole. The sudden dark pressed on the cockpit glass like a weight. Only the faint glow of molten veins deep in the fragment's stone gave the interior shape. Jagged walls loomed close, lined with crystals that caught the Fortune's running lights and sent them back in broken rainbows.

The ship rattled violently. Kael fought the controls, trying to keep their nose straight. "This place is a coffin."

"Not if we follow the current," Liora said.

"What current? All I see are rocks waiting to chew us in half."

She lifted her staff and touched the deck. A pulse went out, faint at first, then stronger. The cavern answered. The walls shimmered, a low vibration running through the stone. The map's projection shifted, showing a narrow spiral path leading deeper into the hollow.

Kael swore under his breath, but angled the Fortune's nose toward it. The ship dipped and banked through the spiral, scraping so close to stone that sparks sprayed across the viewport.

Behind them, the Order's hunters slipped into the cavern mouth. Their pale engines burned steady, their hulls cutting the dark like knives. Kael's stomach tightened.

"They'll follow us anywhere," he muttered.

"They cannot follow everywhere," Liora replied.

The spiral tightened. Kael gritted his teeth and rolled the ship through a gap barely wider than the Fortune's wingspan. A long shard of crystal screeched along the hull. Warning glyphs flared red.

"They'll cut us apart in here," Kael growled.

"Trust," Liora said. Her voice was calm, but sweat glistened on her brow. She leaned forward, her eyes shut, the staff trembling in her grip.

The air grew colder. Kael could feel it in his bones, as if the cavern itself were sucking the heat from his blood. Then, in the distance, he saw it—an opening, a shaft that led deeper down, where a faint blue glow pulsed like the beat of a heart.

Liora's eyes snapped open. "There!"

Kael shoved the throttle. The Fortune roared down the shaft. The walls blurred into streaks. Behind them, one of the Order's ships clipped the stone. The detonation lit the cavern in a flash of pale fire. Fragments rained down, smashing into the others.

Kael whooped, breathless. "Ha! That's one less—"

The smile died on his lips. The remaining two hunters were still on their tail, slipping through the wreckage without pause.

The shaft opened suddenly into a vast hollow chamber, the size of a city, its ceiling lost in shadow. A massive crystalline formation hung in the center, glowing faint blue, veins of power running through it like frozen lightning. The glow pulsed in time with Kael's heartbeat.

"What in the hells is that?" Kael whispered.

Liora's voice was hushed, reverent. "The core of a Shard. Dead, but not silent. It remembers."

The Order's ships poured into the chamber behind them.

Kael jerked the controls, dodging fire. Blue lances tore past, shattering chunks of floating stone. He dove toward the crystal, weaving through spires jutting like teeth.

"Now would be a good time for another miracle!" he shouted.

Liora slammed her staff to the deck. The hum that followed was deeper, resonating with the massive core itself. The crystal answered, its glow flaring bright.

A shockwave tore through the chamber. The Fortune bucked hard, thrown like a toy. Kael wrestled the controls, teeth bared. Behind them, the two hunters faltered. Their hulls scraped stone. One was torn apart in an explosion of shards and fire. The other spun wildly, struck by a crystal spire, and vanished into the dark.

Silence followed. Only the hum of the crystal filled the chamber.

Kael sagged in his chair, chest heaving. "Tell me that was you."

Liora's face was pale, lips trembling, but she held herself upright. "Not me. The Shard. It lent me its voice."

Kael looked at the glowing mass, still pulsing like a heart. For a moment, he could almost believe it was alive.

The map flickered again, brighter now than ever. A new path extended outward from the Shard's core, deeper into the Drift.

Kael stared at it, jaw tight. He wanted to turn back, sell the capsule, forget all of this. But he knew there was no going back. Not anymore.

He glanced at Liora. Her eyes were closed again, but she was smiling faintly, as if she had heard something beautiful.

Kael tightened his grip on the controls. "All right," he muttered. "Let's see where this cursed thing wants to take us."

The Fortune turned, nose tilting toward the new path. The glow of the Shard faded behind them, replaced by the endless dark of the Drift.

ACT II – Fire in the Belt

Chapter 10 – Riftborn Raid

The Drift stretched on like a wound in the sky.

Kael Veyra sat hunched over the *Wraith's Fortune's* console, eyes red from too little sleep, one hand tapping nervously on the throttle housing. The map capsule pulsed faintly in his jacket pocket, as though reminding him it was still there, still leading them deeper into places no sane pilot would fly.

He hated it. He hated the silence between star systems, the way the sensors lied, the way distance and scale twisted until nothing could be trusted. He hated most of all the knowledge that something was always hunting them.

Liora sat in the co-pilot seat with her eyes closed, staff laid across her lap, her breathing steady. If she felt fear, she did not show it.

Kael glanced at her and scowled. "How do you do that?"

She opened her eyes. "Do what?"

"Sit there like a stone while we're one blown coil away from being scrap."

Her lips curved in a faint smile. "Stones endure. That is the lesson."

"Stones also crack and kill everyone standing on them," Kael muttered. He reached over the console, slapped a flickering screen, and sighed when it steadied.

The ship shuddered suddenly, a tremor that ran through the hull. Kael froze. His eyes darted to the scopes. No signatures. No power spikes. Just the same broken debris field they had been drifting through for hours.

Then the lights cut out.

The *Fortune* dropped into blackness. Emergency glyphs blinked red across the console. Kael swore. "Not now—"

The hull rang with a heavy metallic *clang*. Then another. Then three at once.

"They've latched on," Kael whispered.

Liora's eyes widened. "Who?"

The answer came before Kael could speak. A torch flared outside the viewport, burning a circle through the ship's side. Sparks showered. Metal screamed. With a final pop, a section of the hull fell inward, glowing red at the edges.

Figures poured through the breach, armored in patchwork plating, their helmets crowned with shards of bone and steel. The Riftborn.

Kael leapt from the chair, blaster in hand. The first pirate through raised a crude shotgun. Kael shot him square in the chest. The body crumpled, but two more replaced him instantly.

Liora rose, staff humming. She slammed it against the deck. A pulse of resonance shook the air, sending a ripple through the pirates. One staggered back, clutching his helmet. Another dropped his weapon.

Kael fired again, then ducked as a bolt scorched the bulkhead over his head. "Great," he shouted. "Your friends came to say hello!"

"I am not Riftborn," Liora snapped. She swung her staff, catching a pirate's wrist with a burst of vibration that shattered his weapon.

The fight spilled into the narrow corridor. Pirates snarled behind their masks, shouting in a guttural dialect. One lunged at Kael with a jagged blade. Kael blocked with his blaster, kicked the man's knee, and fired point-blank into his chest.

Still more came. The ship echoed with boots and gunfire.

Kael felt the blood drain from his face. "There's too many. They're boarding us from both sides."

Liora planted herself in the center of the corridor, staff glowing brighter now. "Then stand with me."

For a moment, Kael considered running for the escape pod, leaving her and the cursed capsule behind. But something in the way she stood — unflinching, calm even as fire sparked around them — stopped him.

He gritted his teeth, reloaded, and took position at her side. "Fine. But if I die, I'm haunting you."

The next wave of pirates surged forward.

Blaster fire turned the narrow corridor into a furnace of light and noise. Kael crouched low, firing quick, dirty shots. He had no time to aim, no time to breathe. The *Fortune* shuddered with every hit, and he could almost feel her ribs buckling.

A pirate lunged at him from the flank, jagged blade raised high. Kael twisted, fired blind, and the man's body slammed into the bulkhead. Another came, swinging a length of chain. Kael ducked just in time. The chain sparked across the wall, inches from his skull.

Liora's staff hummed louder, its crystal vibrating until Kael's teeth ached. She spun it in her hands, the air trembling with each strike. When she slammed it to the deck again, a wave of resonance blasted outward. The pirates staggered, ears ringing, weapons clattering to the floor.

But still they came.

Kael spat sweat from his mouth and ducked behind a sparking conduit. "You can't keep rattling them forever!"

Liora's voice was calm but strained. "I do not need forever. Only long enough."

"Long enough for what—"

The ship's lights snapped back on. Emergency glyphs flashed bright. The *Fortune*'s engines roared to life. Kael's eyes widened. Someone was flying her.

A voice boomed through the comm, harsh and guttural. "This ship is claimed by the Riftborn. Cease resistance, or we open her spine and let the void take you."

Kael's stomach dropped. That voice. He knew it.

The pirates halted their advance, weapons still raised but steady now. Liora glanced at Kael. "Who is that?"

Kael clenched his jaw. "Trouble."

The comm crackled again. "Kael Veyra. We know your scent. You abandoned the clans, sold us out to Meridian dogs. Today, you answer."

Kael froze. Every instinct screamed at him to deny it, to shoot his way clear, to run. But he knew the truth of those words. The Riftborn did not forgive.

The corridor filled with silence, broken only by the hum of Liora's staff. The pirates tightened their formation. They were not just here for plunder. They were here for him.

"Drop your weapon," one snarled through his helmet. "Or we gut the priestess and throw her into space."

Liora lifted her chin, unafraid. "They will not harm me. They fear the Shards too much."

Kael cursed under his breath. He hated her calm certainty. He hated that she was probably right.

Slowly, he lowered his blaster.

The pirates moved fast, wrenching it from his grip and shoving him to his knees. Rough hands yanked Liora's staff away and bound her wrists with magnetic cuffs. She did not resist.

Kael's chest burned with humiliation as they dragged him toward the breach. He caught glimpses of his ship's scarred walls, his ship that had carried him through a hundred escapes, now crawling with scavengers like carrion birds.

The airlock opened. Beyond, a Riftborn boarding craft clung to the hull, its metal spines digging deep like a parasite. The stench of smoke and oil poured out.

The pirates shoved Kael and Liora inside. The hatch slammed shut.

The boarding craft was a pit of rust and shadows. Nets hung from the ceiling, holding scraps of metal and bone trophies. The floor vibrated with the thrum of an old reactor.

At the far end stood a man Kael knew too well. Broad shoulders, armor pieced together from a dozen battles, helmet shaped with a jagged crest of bone. When he pulled it off, the face beneath was scarred, one eye replaced by a burning red implant.

"Kael Veyra," he growled. "The traitor returns."

Kael forced a grin, though his stomach churned. "Good to see you too, Jorren. Still running this rust heap, I see."

The war-captain of the Riftborn sneered. "Still running from debts, I see." He stepped closer, the implant eye whirring. "You cost us blood. You sold a run to Meridian. Half my crew burned because of you."

Kael's throat tightened. He remembered the screams, the fire, the way he'd run. He pushed the memory down. "That was a long time ago."

"Not long enough." Jorren backhanded him hard. Kael's head snapped to the side. Blood filled his mouth.

Liora stepped forward despite her cuffs. "He is not the same man you knew. The Shards have called him—"

Jorren's laugh was harsh. "A priestess? You travel with holy liars now, Kael? You've fallen further than I thought." He turned to his men. "Chain him. We'll drag him back to the clans. Let them decide if his blood buys back our dead."

The pirates cheered.

Kael spat blood onto the deck. His grin was gone now. He looked at Liora, and for the first time, he saw no calm in her eyes. Only fear — not for herself, but for him.

The chains closed around his wrists.

And Kael knew Act II had begun.

Chapter 11 – Trial by Fire

The Riftborn carried Kael and Liora into the heart of their flagship, a gutted freighter reforged into something uglier. Its corridors were lined with scorched plating, trophies of shattered ships welded to the walls. The air stank of smoke, oil, and sweat.

Kael's wrists burned from the manacles. Each step rattled the chain between them. Behind, two guards prodded him forward with shock-pikes. Ahead, Jorren walked with his head high, the bone crest on his armor glowing faintly in the ship's light.

The chamber they entered was wide and circular, lit by braziers that spat oily flame. A hundred Riftborn filled the space, standing shoulder to shoulder. Their armor was piecemeal, their helmets crowned with jagged metal and bone. The air was alive with their guttural chanting, a rhythm that grew louder as Kael was shoved into the circle.

Liora was forced to her knees beside him. Her staff was gone. Her robes were dirty, cuffs biting into her wrists, but her back was straight and her eyes calm.

Jorren raised his arms. The chanting ceased at once.

"Brothers, sisters," his voice thundered, amplified by the chamber's walls. "A ghost has returned to us. A traitor who sold our blood to the Accord. Who left us burning in Meridian guns."

A roar filled the room. Weapons banged against shields. Sparks leapt from metal on metal.

Jorren grabbed Kael by the hair, forcing his face up to the crowd. "Kael Veyra. Once of the clans. Now a coward and a liar. Tell them, smuggler. Tell them what you did."

Kael's jaw clenched. The memory flashed unbidden: fire, screaming voices, the cargo bay filling with smoke as he sealed the hatch and ran. The faces of the men who'd trusted him. He could still hear them pounding on the bulkhead.

He wanted to deny it. He wanted to spit in Jorren's face and call him a liar. But when he looked up at the crowd, at their eyes burning with rage, he knew it was useless.

"I made a deal," he said. His voice was hoarse. "Meridian wanted the run. I gave it to them. You paid the price."

The chamber erupted. Shouts of *traitor*, *coward*, *blood for blood*.

Jorren let Kael drop to the floor. "You hear it. They know what you are. You will be judged in the old way. By fire."

Two guards dragged Kael toward the center of the circle. There, a pit burned with a strange blue flame, fueled by shard-dust. The heat licked his skin even from meters away.

"Throw him in!" a voice shouted.

"Burn him!"

Kael's heart hammered. He struggled against the guards, but the chains cut his wrists raw. He could feel the heat on his face. He had escaped a hundred traps, cheated a hundred deaths, but this — this was the end.

Then Liora spoke.

"Stop."

Her voice was not loud, but it carried through the chamber like a clear bell. Every Riftborn froze. Even Jorren turned.

She rose to her feet, the cuffs still binding her wrists. Her eyes glowed faintly in the firelight. "You call him traitor. You call him coward. But the Shards do not. The Shards still carry his name."

The Riftborn murmured. Jorren's face darkened. "Lies. Pretty priestess words. They do not matter here."

"They do," Liora said. She stepped forward, chains clinking. "You still sing to the fragments, do you not? You still leave offerings in the vents and the caverns. You still listen for their voices. I am Echo. I can hear them more clearly than you. And they tell me Kael's trial is not yours to give. It is theirs."

Silence stretched. The fire hissed. The Riftborn shifted uneasily, looking to one another.

Jorren sneered. "Prove it."

Liora lifted her bound hands. "Unchain me. Give me the flame. If the Shards deny me, I will burn. If they answer, you will see the truth."

A murmur rippled through the crowd. Some shouted *let her try*. Others cursed her as a liar.

Jorren hesitated. His eye implant whirred as it studied her, calculating. Then, slowly, he gestured.

The guards unlocked her cuffs. Her wrists were red and raw, but she held them steady.

Liora stepped to the pit. The blue flames licked upward, hungry. She closed her eyes and placed her palms over the fire.

The chamber held its breath.

Kael struggled against his chains. "Liora—"

She ignored him.

The flames bent toward her hands. The shard-dust roared brighter, filling the chamber with blinding light. The crowd gasped.

Then the fire stilled. It coiled around her palms, wrapping her wrists like glowing bracelets, and did not burn her.

When she opened her eyes, the blue fire reflected in them. "The Shards speak. Kael's life is not yours to take."

A hush fell. The Riftborn lowered their weapons. Some knelt.

Jorren's face twisted with fury. But even he could not deny what every man and woman in that chamber had seen.

"The Shards have given him back to you," Liora said. Her voice carried like wind over stone. "And if they demand his blood, it will not be here. Not today."

The flames guttered, dimmed, and returned to their normal blue. Liora lowered her hands. Her skin was unmarked.

The Riftborn broke into a roar, not of anger, but awe. They pounded weapons against armor, chanting her name.

Jorren's jaw tightened. He stepped forward, so close Kael could see the twitch in his scar. "Very well. The Shards have spoken. But smuggler..." He leaned close, his breath hot and metallic. "You are not forgiven. You walk with us now. One wrong step, and I will finish what the fire did not."

The guards yanked Kael upright, dragging him back from the pit. His heart still hammered, his throat raw, but he could breathe. He looked at Liora. She stood tall, her hands still faintly glowing, eyes steady on his.

For the first time, Kael felt something he had not felt in years. Not fear. Not guilt.

Hope.

Chapter 12 – Fragile Trust

The Riftborn flagship drifted through the Drift like a scar across the void. Its engines spat a steady trail of smoke and shard-fire, pulling the raiding flotilla behind it in ragged formation. From a distance the convoy looked like a chain of scavenged beasts lashed together, ready to tear apart anything unlucky enough to cross their path.

Kael Veyra stood chained near the prow of the observation deck, staring at the wreckage of dead ships drifting by. The Riftborn loved their trophies, and this deck was lined with them: hull plates carved with scorch marks, the broken spine of a fighter, bones strung into crude banners. The smell of oil and burnt metal clung to every surface.

He hated it. Not just the stink or the noise of the Riftborn chanting below decks. He hated being back here. This was his past, the life he had clawed his way out of. And now, somehow, he was chained to it again.

Liora stood beside him, wrists still raw from the shackles. The Riftborn treated her with wary awe now, giving her space, but never letting her forget she was a prisoner. She gazed out at the stars with calm eyes, though Kael could see the exhaustion in her posture. Her hands trembled faintly whenever she thought no one was looking.

"You saved my life," Kael said at last. His voice was rough, the words harder than he expected. "Back in the pit. You could've let them burn me."

Liora glanced at him. "The Shards spared you. I only spoke their will."

He laughed without humor. "You really believe that, don't you?"

"I do." She tilted her head. "Don't you?"

Kael turned away, jaw tight. He wanted to say no, that it was all smoke and lies. But the image of the fire bending to her hands was burned into his memory. He had seen tricks before. That had not been one.

Before he could answer, Jorren strode onto the deck. The Riftborn captain's scarred face glistened in the firelight. His implant eye whirred as it focused on Kael.

"Walk," Jorren growled.

Two guards unlocked Kael's chains and shoved him forward. Liora made to follow, but Jorren held up a hand. "Not you, priestess. You've already meddled enough. This is clan business."

The guards dragged Kael down the corridors, past chanting Riftborn sharpening weapons and painting bone crests. They threw him into a dim chamber that stank of oil and blood. Jorren entered behind him, sealing the hatch.

The war-captain circled Kael slowly, predator's patience in every step. "You should have died in that fire. Your blood would have washed my hands clean of your betrayal. But the clans saw something in you. Or in her." He spat. "I don't trust it."

Kael rubbed his wrists, keeping his face impassive. "What do you want from me, Jorren? Another confession? Fine. I sold you out. I ran. I'm not proud of it, but I did what I had to. You'd have done the same."

"No." Jorren's voice was a snarl. "I would have died with my clan. That is the difference between us." He leaned close, his scarred face inches from Kael's. "You are alive because of her. Not because you earned it. Remember that."

He slammed a heavy hand against Kael's chest, shoving him back against the wall. Then he dropped something at Kael's feet. A dagger, its hilt wrapped in bone.

"Prove yourself," Jorren said. "Kill her."

Kael's blood ran cold.

Jorren's implant eye whirred. "The priestess is dangerous. She bends fire, sways clans. She'll turn the Riftborn against themselves. End her now, and maybe I'll believe you still have some loyalty left."

Kael stared at the dagger. His heart pounded. He could almost feel the weight of the capsule in his pocket, burning against his chest. The Riftborn wouldn't hesitate to kill Liora once she outlived her usefulness. And Jorren was giving him an easy way out.

If he killed her, he could win his place back. He could save his own skin.

His hand twitched toward the dagger.

But then he remembered the fire. The way it had bent to her palms. The way she had stood before a hundred armed warriors and saved him without fear. The way she had looked at him after, steady, as if she believed there was something in him worth saving.

Kael clenched his fists.

He looked up at Jorren, his jaw set. "If you want her dead, you do it yourself."

Jorren's good eye narrowed. The chamber was silent, save for the hum of the ship's reactor. Then, slowly, Jorren's lips curved into a cruel smile.

"Good," he said. "At least you still have a spine." He picked up the dagger and slid it back into his belt. "But don't mistake defiance for strength, Kael. I'll be watching you. The first time she falters, the first time you falter, I'll put both of you out the airlock."

The hatch slammed open. Guards dragged Kael back toward the deck.

When they threw him down beside Liora again, she looked at him with calm eyes. She said nothing. She didn't need to. Kael knew she had guessed what had happened in that chamber.

And for the first time in years, Kael felt ashamed of the choice he almost made.

Chapter 13 – The Riftborn's Price

The Riftborn fleet fell upon their prey with the hunger of wolves.

Kael stood strapped into the crash seat of a boarding craft, wrists bound to the harness, the rattle of old engines vibrating through his bones. Across from him, Riftborn warriors beat their weapons against their armor in a rhythm that rose and fell like thunder. Sparks leapt from the bulkhead with every strike. The smell of grease and sweat thickened the air.

Beside him sat Liora, her staff still confiscated, her wrists chained. Her face was calm as ever, but Kael saw the tension in her jaw, the way her fingers twitched against the metal cuffs.

Jorren loomed at the front of the craft, one hand gripping a rail overhead, the other resting casually on the bone-handled dagger at his belt. His voice carried over the roar of the engines.

"Today we raid for the clans! Meridian convoys fat with ore and grain. They think the bridges protect them. They think tariffs buy safety. We'll show them the truth: only fear binds the Shards!"

The Riftborn howled their approval.

Kael shifted uncomfortably. He had run raids like this once, years ago. He remembered the rush, the adrenaline, the weight of a blade in his hand. He also remembered the aftermath: bodies cooling in airless holds, the stink of burnt flesh.

Liora leaned close. Her voice was low, meant only for him. "You've done this before."

Kael didn't look at her. "Yeah."

"You hated it."

He smirked bitterly. "Hate's not the word. Survived it. That's all."

The boarding craft shook violently. Warning glyphs flashed red. Jorren grinned. "Target sighted. Meridian freighter. Shields low. Easy prey!"

The craft slammed against the freighter's hull with a bone-jarring crash. Magnets clamped. Torches flared, cutting a glowing circle into the metal. The Riftborn roared as the breach fell inward, and they poured through like a flood.

Kael's restraints were cut. A rifle shoved into his hands. Jorren's voice snarled in his ear. "Fight, traitor. Prove you still bleed Riftborn."

Kael's gut clenched. He raised the rifle, the weight of it heavy, familiar, hated.

They stormed into the freighter's corridor. Meridian crew scrambled for cover, firing pistols that sparked uselessly against the Riftborn's heavy plating. The air filled with smoke and screams.

Kael ducked behind a bulkhead. His hands trembled on the rifle. He could hear Liora behind him, refusing to take a weapon, her eyes following everything.

A young Meridian officer stumbled into view, blaster shaking in his hands. Kael's reflexes took over. He raised the rifle, finger brushing the trigger.

But he froze.

The officer was barely more than a boy. Terrified. His uniform too big for his frame. Kael saw himself in that fear, years ago, before he'd learned how to kill without thinking.

His finger tightened—then he jerked the rifle upward. The shot scorched harmlessly into the ceiling.

The boy ran.

Jorren's voice thundered behind him. "Coward!"

Kael spun, aiming down the corridor. He fired again, this time at a cluster of crates above two Riftborn. They crashed down, blocking the passage. The freighter crew scrambled into the opening, fleeing deeper into the ship.

Kael shouted over the chaos, "Go! Run!"

The Meridian crew vanished into the smoke.

Jorren shoved Kael hard against the wall. His implant eye burned red. "You let them live."

Kael's heart hammered. He bared his teeth. "I helped you take the ship. You wanted proof, you got it."

Jorren's lip curled. "Proof of weakness." He raised the dagger, pressing its tip against Kael's throat. "Next time, I cut you myself."

"Then do it," Kael spat. "But you'll never get your Shards to sing for you."

For a heartbeat Kael thought Jorren would slit his throat then and there. Instead, the war-captain snarled and shoved him away.

The Riftborn secured the freighter, dragging prisoners into chains, stripping cargo holds. The raid was theirs.

But Kael had made his choice. He had spared lives, and in doing so, drawn a line in the blood and smoke.

Later, as the boarding craft rattled back toward the Riftborn flagship, Liora leaned close again. Her voice was soft, but there was steel in it.

"You could have killed him. You didn't."

Kael's chest tightened. "Don't read too much into it. I'm just tired of blood."

"No," Liora said. She studied his face, her eyes calm but piercing. "You're beginning to change. The Shards know it. I see it too."

Kael looked away, scowling, but the truth of her words settled into him like a weight.

He wasn't the same man who had run all those years ago.

And Jorren knew it.

Chapter 14 – Echoes in the Dark

The Riftborn flotilla drifted in the shadow of a hollow Shard. The fragment was vast, its jagged edges catching the pale light of the dying sun, its hollow interior pocked with cavern mouths. The fleet hung there like carrion birds circling a carcass.

Kael stood on the observation deck, hands braced against the railing. Below, the Riftborn celebrated their raid with fire and song. They beat drums fashioned from engine housings, roasted stolen meat over shard-flames, and bellowed their victories into the void. To anyone else, it was terrifying. To Kael, it was familiar, too familiar, and the familiarity made his stomach twist.

Liora stood apart from the chaos, gazing out toward the Shard. Her expression was distant, troubled. She seemed not to see the Riftborn or the fires or the trophies. She was listening, though not with her ears.

Kael approached her. "You're doing that thing again," he muttered.

"What thing?"

"Going all glassy-eyed and hearing ghosts."

She didn't look at him. "They are not ghosts. They are memories. The Shards remember what they were. Sometimes they share what they know."

Kael rubbed his temple. "Great. And what are they whispering now?"

Liora finally turned to him. Her eyes glowed faintly in the dim light. "Pain. And warning."

Kael frowned. "That doesn't sound good."

"It isn't." She gripped the railing, her knuckles white. "There is something here. Something old. Buried in the hollow. I can feel it stirring."

Kael glanced at the Shard's looming shadow. "Stirring? What kind of something?"

Liora shook her head. "I don't know. But it was left here for a reason."

Before Kael could reply, Jorren's heavy boots rang against the deck. The Riftborn war-captain strode toward them, his implant eye glowing red in the firelight.

"You feel it too, priestess," Jorren said, his voice a growl. "The hollow sings. The clans have heard its voice for generations. We call it the Black Maw. Ships vanish inside and do not return. Some say the Shard itself eats them."

Liora's gaze didn't falter. "Not the Shard. Something within it."

Jorren's scarred mouth twisted into a cruel smile. "Then we'll claim it. Whatever lies in that hollow belongs to the Riftborn."

He turned, barking orders. A dozen warriors armed themselves and began preparing boarding skiffs. The flotilla stirred with anticipation.

Kael grabbed Jorren's arm. "You can't just march into some cursed cave because it 'sings.' That's suicide."

Jorren shoved him back. "Stay out of this, smuggler. You've already proved you've gone soft. If you won't fight for us, then at least watch and learn how real warriors claim their destiny."

Kael bit back a retort, fists clenched. Liora stepped closer to him, her voice low. "He cannot hear the truth. But we can."

"What truth?" Kael asked.

Her eyes darkened. "That whatever lies in that hollow isn't meant to be claimed. It is meant to be sealed."

The Riftborn skiffs launched, streaking toward the hollow's mouth. Liora insisted on boarding one, her presence demanded by the clans who now regarded her with wary reverence after the fire-pit. Kael, still bound by chains of suspicion, was dragged along at Jorren's command.

The skiff rattled through the hollow's entrance. Darkness swallowed them. Lights flickered on, beams cutting through dust and drifting ice. The cavern stretched vast and silent, walls glittering with crystal veins that pulsed faintly, like a heartbeat.

Liora's breath caught. She pressed her palm against the air, as though feeling through the void itself. "It's alive."

Kael frowned. "Alive? Stones don't live."

"They do when they remember."

The skiff descended deeper. Shapes emerged from the dark—wrecks of ships, dozens of them, tangled together like bones in a mass grave. Riftborn warriors muttered prayers under their breath. Jorren sneered but his grip on his weapon tightened.

At the cavern's heart stood a spire of crystal unlike any Kael had ever seen. Black and jagged, it rose from the floor to the ceiling, veins of faint light crawling through it like veins under skin. The air around it vibrated. Kael felt it in his teeth, in his skull.

Liora went pale. "It's a Shard-heart. But twisted."

Kael squinted. "What does that mean?"

"It means this fragment's core was corrupted when the world broke. Its memory curdled. Its song isn't warning. It's hunger."

As if in answer, the crystal pulsed. A shockwave rippled through the cavern. The wrecked ships stirred, metal groaning, drifting upward as if pulled by invisible strings.

The Riftborn roared in alarm. Weapons fired, bolts sparking off wreckage.

Kael grabbed Liora's arm. "Time to leave."

But Liora's eyes were fixed on the spire, wide with fear and awe. "No. We can't leave it. If it wakes fully, it will devour more than just this Shard. It will spread."

Another pulse struck. This time, Kael felt it in his chest like a second heartbeat. His vision blurred. The map capsule in his jacket grew hot against his skin.

He gasped. "It's connected to the capsule."

Liora's gaze snapped to him. "Then this is only the beginning."

The spire pulsed again, brighter, stronger. The wrecks began to move, slowly, like limbs finding muscle again. Shapes tore free of the twisted ships, limbs of metal and shard-crystal, assembling themselves into something that should not exist.

Kael's blood turned cold. "Tell me that's not what I think it is."

"It's an echo of the Engine," Liora whispered. "A broken piece. A memory trying to become real."

The cavern shook. The Riftborn opened fire. The air filled with screams.

Kael clutched his rifle, heart hammering. He'd wanted out of this life. He'd wanted nothing but credits and freedom. But staring at the spire, at the nightmare taking shape, he knew he was standing at the edge of something far worse than warlords or assassins.

The Shards were not just broken.

They were waking.

Chapter 15 – The Hollow Awakens

The cavern shook as if a giant had turned in its sleep. Metal groaned in long, miserable notes. The black crystal spire pulsed again, brighter this time, and the air filled with a taste like cold iron on the tongue.

Jorren braced his boots on the skiff's deck and bellowed orders. Riftborn loosed volleys into the dark, bolts cracking against drifting wreckage and the rising limbs of something that was not a ship at all. The wrecks flexed and folded as if remembering joints. A rib cage of plating bent inward. A cluster of engine bells clenched into a false heart. The thing that took shape had no single outline, only intent.

Liora swayed where she stood, one hand on the skiff's rail, the other lifted toward the spire. Her pupils were blown wide. The veins in her throat stood out with strain.

"Liora," Kael said. "Tell me you have a plan."

"It is remembering the wrong self," she whispered. "I need to make it remember the right one."

"Translate," Kael snapped.

"Resonance," she said, teeth clenched. "It is singing hunger. I can answer with a different tone. I need a louder voice."

Jorren stabbed a finger toward the thing assembling in the air. "Louder will not help if it eats us first. Fire on the joints. Bring it down."

Riftborn obeyed. Bolts struck the thing's seamlines. Shards flew. The mass reknit itself and reached with a crooked arm. A skiff came apart like thin tin in its grasp. Screams cut off at once. The arm dropped the wreck and reached for another.

Kael's eyes flicked to the skiff's control panel. Old Meridian hardware under a coat of grime. Comms coils. A salvage winch with a grav inductor the size of his forearm. He grabbed a panel tool from a crate and jammed it under the console's lip.

Jorren rounded on him. "What do you think you are doing."

"Stealing your ship for five minutes," Kael said. "You can have it back if we live."

Jorren reached for him. Liora's voice cut through, thin but steady. "Let him."

Kael ripped the panel open. The guts of the skiff looked like everything else Riftborn built. Functional, half cursed, wire looms braided with leather. He found the inductor line by feel and yanked it free. The deck listed. The winch motor squealed.

"Jorren," Kael said without looking up. "You want that thing to stop. I need your coils and I need you to point the nose at the spire."

Jorren's scar twitched. For a breath Kael thought he would order Kael shot and be done. Then the war-captain shoved a pilot aside and shouldered into the helm. The skiff swung until the spire filled the view.

Liora watched the black crystal with the focus of a drowning woman watching a distant shore. "Bring the coil to me."

Kael hauled the thick cable across the deck. It rose warm under his palms, buzzing with captive force. He clipped the leads to the iron ring at the base of Liora's cuffs, the only metal left on her person. The cable throbbed against his wrist.

"This will burn," he said.

"Then it will be honest," she said, and lifted her hands.

The coil lit her bones from inside. The hum of her staff was gone, but the new note that filled the skiff was cleaner, colder, a thread of sound you felt in your teeth and the cartilage of your nose. The black spire answered with a deeper beat. For a heartbeat the two tones fought like dogs. Then, very slowly, Liora's note slid under the other, caught it, and turned it.

The thing of wreckage spasmed. The false ribs loosened. The engine heart stuttered like a misfiring pump.

"It is working," Kael said. His voice came out hoarse.

"For now," Liora said. Her face had gone very pale. Sweat ran from her hairline into her eyes. "It will not hold. There are anchors feeding it. Three, maybe four. Break them, or it will relearn the hunger."

"Where," Jorren demanded.

Liora turned her head a fraction, as if listening to the cavern walls. "Not eyes. Hands. Kael, the capsule."

He did not ask how she knew. He plunged his hand into his jacket and slapped the relic onto the console. It woke with a shock of cold. Light spilled in thin lines, not a star map this time, but a ghostly overlay of the cavern itself. Veins of pale blue ran through the stone like frost. Three bright nodes pulsed at equal distances around the spire.

Kael stabbed at the nearest with a finger. "There. There. And there."

"Take charges," Jorren barked, already moving. "Two teams with me. Two with the smuggler. The rest hold the line and keep that thing busy."

Kael grabbed a bandolier from a locker, checked the charges by habit, and slung them across his chest. He hooked the coil free of Liora and pressed the capsule into her hand.

"Can you keep that tone without the coil," he asked.

Her hands trembled. "I must. If it shifts, run."

"Not helpful," Kael said, but he managed a crooked smile. "Keep singing."

He clipped on mag boots and jumped. The cavern's gravity was a mess of suggestions and lies. He fell sideways, then down, then his boots caught a plate of old hull. He ran across it, leaped to a spar of crystal, and pulled himself along hand over hand. Behind him Jorren and four Riftborn followed with a competence that irritated Kael more than it should have.

The first anchor node rose from the cavern floor like a thorn. It was not clean crystal. It had metal veined through it, plates half fused and half grown, a cancer of memory. The hum here was thicker. Kael felt it drag on his lungs.

He thumbed a charge and wedged it into a fault line. He should have stepped back at once. He found himself watching the way the faint light crawled in the crystal, thinking of veins under skin.

"Move," Jorren snapped.

Kael shook himself and kicked off. The charge's timer blinked a patient red. Kael and Jorren tumbled away, caught an outcrop, and flattened themselves as the shock rolled through the stone. The anchor node cracked. Light leaked from the break like breath.

The thing in the air jerked as if struck across the face. A beam of bolted plates fell away and spun into the dark.

"Good," Jorren said, a savage grin cutting his scars. "Two more."

They ran the rim of the chamber. The second node reared above a forest of twisted trusses. Riftborn bolts flashed past as the holding teams kept the wreck beast occupied. Kael wetted his lips and ignored the way his hands shook. The hum underfoot rose in pitch, angry now, no longer purely hungry.

He set the second charge. The timer counted. He and Jorren moved, late by a heartbeat, and the blast picked them up and threw them into a tumble that stole breath and sense. Kael slammed into a floating girder. His shoulder went hot with pain. Stars went gray and then came back.

A hand closed on his harness and dragged him level. Jorren, face set, breath harsh, shoved him toward the third anchor.

"We are not done until it is done," Jorren said. "Do not die before that."

"Look at us," Kael panted. "Working together. Miracles everywhere."

They scrambled. The third node sat in a pocket of the wall that looked like an old wound. The crystal there had a darker sheen, almost oily. Kael did not like the feel of it, and he liked what the capsule showed him even less. The node was thicker, brighter, greedy with current.

The wreck thing saw them. A limb of stitched beams swung wide. Bolts sparked off it to little effect. It came on, steady and wrong.

Jorren set his stance, lifted a launcher, and fired a rocket into the limb at a joint where old plating overlapped new. The blast sheared the joint. The arm drifted, then swung back on cables, grasping for purchase. Jorren tossed the empty tube and grabbed fresh charges from Kael's bandolier without asking.

"Plant and go," he said.

Kael jammed a charge into a tight seam. The timer blinked faster than the others. The anchor felt more awake. He set a second for certainty. His hands wanted to shake. He told them no.

The limb came again, faster now. Jorren stepped into it. He could not stop it, but he could turn it. He dug his mag boots into the crystal and leaned his whole weight against the blow. The arm skidded, scraped sparks, and slammed into the wall above their heads. The shock ran through the stone, through their bones, through their teeth.

"Run," Jorren said, and for once Kael did not argue.

They kicked free, fell along an arc that only made sense because the hum told it to. The shock of the third detonation was different. The cavern did not just shake. It sighed. The black spire flared and then dimmed, as if some great lung had emptied.

The wreck thing folded like a puppet with cut strings. Its false ribs sagged. The engine heart came apart into useless bells. The loose limb that had battered Jorren tumbled away, harmless as trash.

On the skiff, Liora swayed. She had both hands wrapped around the capsule, the light from it running up her veins. Her mouth was open in a soundless note. When the anchors broke, the light in her hands flickered like a candle in wind.

Kael caught the edge of the skiff and hauled himself over the rail. He reached for Liora at the same heartbeat the black spire gave one last pulse, a terrible, lonely beat that made the world thin.

Liora arched like a bowstring. The note in the air turned inside out. The deck lights blew with a pop. The Riftborn nearest her threw up their hands and fell to their knees without knowing why.

Kael grabbed Liora's shoulders. Her skin burned his palms. He did not let go.

"Stop," he said. "Come back. You hear me. Come back."

Her eyes focused by degrees. The glow faded. She collapsed against him, light as ash. The capsule fell from her fingers and hit the deck with a sound like a dropped coin. It lay dark for a moment, then woke again in a gentler pulse. A new line had drawn itself on the map. Not into this cavern. Away from it. Deeper.

Jorren loomed over them, one hand on the rail, the other clenched at his side. He stared past them at the spire. Its light had sunk to a sullen ember. The hum in the stone had retreated to a low headache.

"What did you do," he asked. His voice was a rasp.

"We reminded it," Liora said. Her voice was raw. "Not a mouth. A memory. It will not try to become a hunger again. Not soon."

Jorren's implant eye spun and clicked as it recorded. He looked at Kael then, and in his expression there was something like respect, stripped of heat.

"You ran once," Jorren said quietly. "You did not run today."

"New habit," Kael said. He checked Liora's pulse with clumsy fingers. It was there, thin but real. Relief loosened something tight in his chest. "Do not get used to it."

Jorren barked a laugh that had no joy. He jerked his chin at the pilot. "Back to the flotilla. All units, break contact and withdraw. We have pulled the Maw's teeth."

The skiffs turned. The cavern shifted. The collapse did not come at once. It came in small choices. A cradled wreck lost its balance and drifted into a spar. The spar cracked and fell into a ring of girders that had been waiting to remember gravity. The ring tipped and slid. Dust rose in glittering sheets.

"Time to go," Kael said.

They went. The skiffs threaded the hollow's throat, engines whining, pilots sweating. A dying chunk of station clipped a hull and spun past. The Riftborn sang again, a different song now, fierce and fast, the kind you use to outrun falling ceilings.

The flotilla broke into open space and fanned outward. The hollow behind them shed a slow tear of debris that spread like a veil.

On the flagship's hangar deck the noise of victory returned at once. Riflebuts hammered hulls. Fires roared in braziers. Bone crests rattled on helmet crowns. Liora did not hear it. She sat on a crate with her eyes closed while a clan healer smoothed salve over the burns on her palms. Kael stood beside her and did not fidget.

Jorren approached with a piece of the black crystal wrapped in wire. It pulsed like a weak heartbeat, throwing a faint, sour light across his scars.

"A trophy," he said. "To prove what we took from the Maw."

"Throw it back," Liora said without opening her eyes. "It is a splinter of the wrong song. Do not bring it among your children."

Jorren's mouth twitched. For a moment it looked like he would hurl the shard into the fire. He did not. He lowered it and wrapped it tighter in the wire.

"I will keep it where it cannot touch anyone," he said. "But I will keep it. We are not afraid of what hurt us."

"You should be respectful of it," Liora said. "Fear is not the only teacher."

Jorren looked at Kael. "Your priestess is brave," he said. "She is also trouble."

"I noticed," Kael said.

"Good," Jorren said. "Keep her from getting herself killed before we have use of her again."

Kael bristled. "She is not yours."

"Neither are you," Jorren said, and for once there was no venom in it. "But for now, you walk with us. The clans will speak of the Maw and of a smuggler who broke anchors with a war-captain he once betrayed. They will not forgive. They will remember. That is something."

He turned away, shouting for a council. The Riftborn flowed toward him, a river of armor and old scars.

Kael looked down at Liora. Her lashes trembled. She opened her eyes and gave him a tired smile.

"You did not let go," she said.

"You told me to trust you," he said. "I thought I should finally try it."

She nodded. "Then hear this. The capsule showed a new path. I saw it when you did. The spire did not only remember itself. It remembered a friend."

Kael frowned. "You mean another hollow."

"I mean a hand reaching from farther in," Liora said. "An echo of what made the Engines in the first place. The Order will feel this. Drax will hear it as gossip. Meridian will call it rumor. But the Shards know. They are waking. If we do not move first, someone else will move for us."

Kael rubbed a thumb across the smooth face of the capsule. The line on its map pulsed, thin and sure. He could feel the old tug in his gut that always came before a bad decision. He looked up and saw, far across the hangar, the bulkhead that framed the door to the bay where the *Wraith's Fortune* waited under guard. He imagined the shape of her in the low light, dented and faithful and ready to run.

"You said we reminded this place," he said. "Can you do it again, if we find another."

"I can try," Liora said. "It will cost."

"Everything worth doing does," Kael said.

Above the hangar, unseen, a ripple of cold moved through the dark like breath drawn in. Sensors on a dozen ships would log it later, argue, dismiss, and file. The Obsidian Order would not argue. They would read it as a signpost. Somewhere in the Belt, a masked head would tilt, and a hunt would turn its nose.

Kael did not feel that ripple, not as a warning. He felt only the small pull between his ribs, the way the map wanted them to go. He offered Liora a hand. She took it and stood, careful of her burns.

"Get some rest," he said. "We fly at shift change. I will talk Jorren into letting us breathe vacuum again."

"You think that will work," she asked.

"I will not ask," Kael said.

He left her with the healer and crossed the hangar to the guards posted at the ramp of the *Fortune*. He had a grin he used for customs officers and difficult bartenders. He put it on like a mask. He did not feel it. He felt tired and strangely light.

He paused on the ramp and looked back. Liora sat straight despite the tremor in her fingers. Jorren stood with his captains, the wrapped shard tucked under his arm, his head bent as if listening to something only he could hear. The Riftborn sang around them, loud and certain and alive.

Kael put his palm against the hull plate by the hatch. The metal throbbed faintly with heat and old, stubborn life. He spoke under his breath so only the ship could hear.

"You and me, girl. One more run. Maybe the worst one yet."

The hatch opened. The *Wraith's Fortune* breathed him in.

Chapter 16 – Meridian Shadows

The bridge glittered like a white river beneath the station windows, steady as a heartbeat, patient as stone. High Warden Seris Thane watched it in silence while the Resolve refueled and the shift bells rolled across Anchor Spindle. On the glass, her reflection looked tired. The streak of white at her temple had lengthened in the last few weeks, a thin flag that would not lie down.

Lieutenant Mara Pell stepped into the ready room with two slates and a face that said the news was bad. Seris already knew it would be.

"Start with the numbers," Seris said.

Mara set a slate on the table. "Four convoys in nine days routed through maintenance arcs. Each one carried relief crates for outer fragments. All four show mass discrepancies. All four came within a hair of our patrol windows. Here are the access logs for schedule edits."

Seris keyed the slate. Names and authorizations scrolled past, too many of them. She felt the little tug in her chest that came before anger and exhaled until it passed.

"Who touched both schedules and manifests," she asked.

Mara showed the second slate. "Three clerks in Port Logistics. Two dock foremen. One council aide, level black. Name redacted. The edits to our patrol windows piggybacked on his clearances."

"Of course they did," Seris said.

"Councilor Venn called while you were in the gym," Mara added. "He wants a public inspection of the Riftborn berths. Cameras, press, the whole parade. He thinks visible force will calm the guilds."

"Visible force will sell headlines," Seris said. "It will also tip anyone who is paying attention that we are short handed. We are not doing theater today."

Mara hesitated. "Then what do we do."

Seris put her palms flat on the table. The metal was cool and honest. "We find the next shipment and we put our hands on it. No comms. No announcements. You, me, six wardens I would trust with my lungs. We take a cutter down to Port Ring Three and we watch a crate move from a dock to a hold. If there is nothing in it, I will write Venn the prettiest apology he has ever received."

Mara's mouth twitched. "And if there is something."

"Then we know exactly which hands turned the key," Seris said.

They moved. Resolve undocked with the smooth grace that came from a crew who could read each other without speaking. Seris took a seat in the forward pit and let the station rotate past in a slow spin of white girders and dock arms. Port Ring Three lay on the shadow side, under the bulk of the spindle. The lighting strips down there had a permanent dusk that Seris had never trusted. Dusk is where people make mistakes on purpose.

The cutter's ramps dropped without fanfare. The eight wardens she had chosen fell into step, visors down, batons low. Seris wore only her sidearm and the short cloak that marked command. She left the cloak folded back. The pistol was visible. She wanted it to be.

They walked a long arc past bulkhead doors and open mouths of storage bays. Dockers leaned on railings and watched them pass. A woman eating an apple tossed the core into a belt of moving trash and did not look away from Seris. That was fine. Seris was not hiding. She had given up on hiding when she took her oath.

Port Logistics sat behind a smoked pane with a comm slot and a bored clerk. The clerk looked up just far enough to make a show of recognition.

"High Warden Thane. What an honor," he said. "Something I can do for the Accord today."

"I need to see manifests and seals for the Anchor Twelve relief outbound in six hours," Seris said. "Now, please."

He tapped a key with theatrical slowness. "Those are sealed at council discretion. I can ask my supervisor to request a release."

"Use your key," Seris said. "Show me the seals. I am not leaving until I see them."

He smiled with his mouth and not his eyes. "I do not have authority."

Seris studied his collar. Silver thread, a half shade cleaner than everyone else's. "You do not need authority to fetch your supervisor. You need legs. Use them."

He swallowed and stood. When the inner door shut behind him, Mara leaned in close.

"We have a tail," Mara said softly. "Back at the pier. Two men in neutral greys. They fell in when we turned down the main corridor."

"Good," Seris said. "Let them watch."

The clerk returned with a woman whose hair was arranged like a sculpture and whose badge bore a cluster of small pins that spoke of committees and dinners Seris would never attend. The woman smiled like a door that has already decided not to open.

"High Warden," she said. "I am Talen Pryce, acting deputy for Venn's office here at Spindle. I understand you have a request."

Seris kept her hands at her sides. "I am here to verify seals on Anchor Twelve relief. Then I am going to follow those crates to the ship that loads them. Then I am going to escort that ship through the bridge. For the optics."

Pryce's smile tightened. "There is no need for that level of involvement. The Accord has processes that work. Your presence would signal distrust."

"It would signal that I do my job," Seris said. "Now, the seals."

Pryce weighed defiance against risk, then flicked a hand. The clerk slid a reader through the slot. Seris placed her palm on the plate. The first list appeared, clean as new snow. Food packets, medkits, cloth. All the right words lined up in all the right order.

"Physical seals," Seris said. "Not the poetry. The tags."

Pryce drew breath the way people do when they want to remind you who owns your salary. Seris turned her head a fraction and let her gaze touch the wardens behind her. Eight visors. Eight batons. Mara with her jaw set. Pryce let the breath out without the speech and nodded once.

They walked the cargo maze in silence. Seris kept her eyes on hands. She trusted hands more than faces. The crates for Anchor Twelve sat in Bay 3-Delta, stacked to shoulder height. The seals were new and unblemished. That meant nothing. Seris slid a tool from her belt and set the head against the corner seam of the top crate. Pryce reached out a hand.

"Warden. Please. We have procedures for inspection. You need a triad of signatures and a union rep and a neutral observer from the guild. If you cut that without them, the council will write you up for violation."

Seris met her gaze and did not blink. "I brought my signatures." She lifted her chin at Mara and the wardens. "I have union support in my pocket, if this crate is what you say it is. And I do not need a neutral observer. I am the neutral observer."

She cut. The seal parted with a soft adhesive sigh. The lid came free. Inside lay rows of white ration bricks and a layer of med patches. Seris lifted a brick, weighed it in her hand, and set it down. It felt honest.

Pryce smiled again. It had more teeth in it this time. "Satisfied."

Seris leaned in and pressed the ration bricks with two fingers. They were glued to a false panel. She slid the tool into the gap and pried. The panel lifted. Beneath the food lay a second layer. Powder blue shells, nested like eggs. Heavy.

Seris took one out. It filled her palm and then some. She recognized the contours. Forge-State microcap rounds. Rifle food for armored troops. She looked at Mara. Mara did not swear, though Seris saw her mouth want to.

Pryce's face went still for a breath, then settled into a careful blank. "I am sure there is an explanation."

"I am sure you will enjoy writing it," Seris said.

Feet scuffed behind them. The two men in neutral greys had come closer. They had shed their indifference like skin. Their jackets hung open over short carbines.

Seris did not turn. She put the shell back into the crate and closed the lid. Her hand did not shake. Her voice did not rise. "Lieutenant. Tag the lot. Quietly. I want chain of custody on every crate. You three, on the pier, eyes open. You three, on the bay doors. Nothing leaves."

She looked at Pryce. "We will speak to Venn. Now."

Pryce's lips moved around something like a smile and found only the shape of fear. She walked, because walking was easier than running when wardens stand behind you.

They used a service comm rather than the polished halo of a council feed. Seris preferred the dirtier channels. They tell the truth more often. Venn arrived in hologram, a pale cylinder resolving into a precise man with careful hair.

"High Warden," he said. "I have a briefing with the guild in eight minutes. If this is about your reluctance to perform a visible inspection of Riftborn berths, we can schedule a discussion for this afternoon."

"This is about weapons," Seris said. "In relief crates. Signed out of Port Logistics. Your aide's key touched the edits that moved my patrol off the blind arc that convoy used last cycle."

Venn's jaw moved once. "That is a serious allegation."

"It is an observation," Seris said. "I am tired of the word allegation. I am tired of projection charts. I am tired of pretending you do not know what moves through your doors."

Pryce found her voice. "Councilor, I can explain."

Venn's eyes cut toward her and back. He did not change expression. "High Warden, stand down. Deliver those crates to Anchor Twelve as scheduled. If there was an error, it is manifest level and it will be corrected in process. We cannot afford a disruption."

Seris felt the old calm settle on her shoulders, the kind you pull on before a storm. "There will be a disruption. I am impounding this cargo. I am impounding the ship it would have boarded. If the captain objects, I will show him the shells and he will stop objecting. If you object, you can come down to Port Ring Three yourself and put your hand on a powder blue round and tell me it is bread."

Venn's gaze went cold. "You are out of line, Thane."

"I am in a line," Seris said. "It stretches from everyone who will die when these rounds are fired to the person who loaded them in this crate. I intend to walk it until I find the end."

He started to speak. She cut the transmission. Mara stared at her as if she had just stepped off a bridge and expected the air to hold her.

"Ma'am," Mara whispered.

"Lock it down," Seris said. "If anyone from Council Security shows up, they can watch from behind my people."

Council Security did not call first. The first warning Seris had was the way conversation changed on the pier, from the indifferent murmur of commerce to the low, tense hiss of men deciding whether to show guns. A narrow man in a black coat walked through the crowd with two uniformed heavies at his back. His badge was clipped to his lapel, the way men clip knives at parties to show they are old enough to be charming.

"Inspector Rallis," he said. "Council Security, internal misappropriation unit. High Warden Thane, you are interfering in a sealed operation. Those crates were to be tracked to a third party. You have compromised a sensitive tail."

Seris had never seen him before, but she knew his type. He was a surgeon who liked to cut. "This is theft," she said. "You are not tracking anything. You are delivering."

Rallis glanced at Mara. "Take your people off the doors, Lieutenant."

Mara's knuckles whitened around her baton. "I take orders from the High Warden."

Rallis smiled. "Not today."

Seris stepped into his space. "The next word out of your mouth had better be a request."

For a heartbeat, Port Ring Three held its breath. Rallis broke the moment with a short laugh. He stepped back and spread his hands.

"Request noted," he said. "Here is mine. Stand down, Thane. Walk away. You burn a lot of colleagues if you push this fast."

"Then they can warm their hands on the report," Seris said.

He studied her face, the way a gambler studies a table that has stopped giving him his luck. He nodded to his heavies. "Record. The High Warden is making an error."

The heavies raised their wrists. Lenses blinked. Seris had no objection to being recorded. She lifted the lid on the crate and held one of the shells up to the lens.

"This is where you are sending bread," she said to the camera. "This is how you buy order. If you want me to carry it for you, come and put it back in my hands."

Rallis's smile never touched his eyes. He nodded, turned, and walked away. Seris felt the tremor that runs through a crowd when a show is over and everyone goes back to their smaller grifts. She exhaled through her teeth. Her shoulders ached as if she had been lifting something heavy for hours.

"Get the crates to the cutter," she said. "Quiet and fast. Rotate the code on the door after each pallet. I want three rings between us and every Council Security feed."

They moved. By the time the last pallet clunked onto the cutter's deck, Seris felt that good tired that comes from clean work. It was the feeling she had joined for. It had been too rare lately.

Resolve slipped her berth with the ease of a ship that knew how to leave without being seen. Seris took the command chair and set the cutter's bay to lock. The shells sat behind steel now. She wanted them out of her ship as soon as possible, but she wanted them to be useful first.

Mara's console chimed. "Incoming, encrypted, your eyes only," she said. "Source masked. The route marker looks like a private node burned through half a dozen relays."

Seris tipped her head. "Put it through."

The voice that came through was thin with compression, but she knew it at once. Kell, the dock rat who had handed her the first chip in a ration wrapper.

"You have proof now," Kell said. No greeting. No titles. "Good. You will want this too. Two hours ago, an Echo Priestess and a smuggler came out of a Riftborn hollow with a vector pointed deeper in. Obsidian ships turned like hounds on a scent. A Forge-State scout picked the rumor off a clan band and sent it to Varak. Meridian analysts flagged it and then buried it. I do not think the burying was an accident."

Seris felt the muscles in her shoulders tighten again, but in a different way. A priestess and a smuggler. The image formed without permission. The bridge-port ambush reports she had skimmed two days ago. A masked assassin on a camera with an image that refused to sharpen. A small battered ship lifting under fire. A woman with a staff stepping into the blast without fear. A man with a gun and a hand that steadied even while he cursed.

"Names," she said.

"Not on the open," Kell said. "But the smuggler used a contact code that smells like the clans. Jorren's clan. You want to help them, tilt your patrol windows twelve degrees and stand off from the Drift belt when you hit your loop. I can keep a Meridian cutter out of their shadow if I have to, but it is cleaner if you do it."

Mara had turned in her chair. Her eyes were bright. "Ma'am."

Seris looked at the bridge. Her crew watched her without watching. They had learned to do that when her decisions had started to sprout teeth.

"Send me your proof chain," Seris said to Kell. "Every relay. Every signature you have on the rumors. If I am going to disobey a council with my ship at my back, I am going to write it into the log with ink that dries hard."

Kell's laugh was short. "You always did like reports. Check your drop in five."

The line died.

Resolve slid along the bridge's inner rail. Seris could have reached out and touched the pylons with her palm from here, or that is how it looked. The light playing along the plasma arcs was harmless as rain behind double glass, and just as deceptive.

Mara stood at her elbow. "If we bend, we give that priestess and her smuggler a shadow to hide in. If we do not, Obsidian runs our lanes and we pretend not to see."

Seris tapped two fingers on the arm of her chair. "We are going to do both. We are going to keep the bridge open and we are going to move the shadow three spans to the left. No notices. No memos. File our patrol change when we are already in the new loop."

Mara grinned, quick and fierce. "Yes, High Warden."

Resolve's engines sang as she eased off the prescribed arc. To anyone with their eyes on a dashboard in a warm office, it looked like a minor correction to avoid a tug. To anyone who had ever flown a cutter in a storm, it looked like a choice.

Seris opened a private channel and set it to spray toward the Drift with a soft pulse that would not travel far. The encryption key she chose was an old one, from a convoy rescue she had run years ago with a wardenship now scrapped for parts. She liked the way the numbers felt under her fingers.

"To the small ship running quiet off Port Ring Three," she said, voice low. "Traffic is heavy to your rear and hungry in front. If you step into the shadow that just opened for you and keep your light down, you will have air to breathe for three hours. Use it to leave less noise than you make. If you do not know who I am, you do not need to. Keep your people alive. That will be enough."

She cut the channel before anyone could answer. She did not want thanks. Thanks complicates.

On the main feed, a council bulletin scrolled. Venn was on a dais, speaking about stability. Hale stood behind him, hands folded, face steady. Sira stood at his other shoulder, eyes bright. The caption ticked past: Meridian ensures relief to the outer fragments despite increased pirate activity. A second caption scrolled under the first, in a smaller font. High Warden Thane to lead public inspection of Riftborn berths this afternoon.

Seris turned the feed off.

Mara watched the now dark pane. "They will come for you," she said. "We both know it."

"They will come for anyone who says no," Seris said. "I am old enough to be bored by that."

She stood and stretched the stiffness out of her shoulders. Resolve purred around her, a metal animal with a good heart. Through the viewport, a freighter eased out of its slot and into the bridge lane. Workers along the spine cramped hands and waved at someone they knew on the deck. A child balanced on a crate and pretended to be a pilot, two fingers out like a nose, eyes wide.

Seris pressed her thumb against the glass. "Keep it open," she said under her breath. "Whatever else breaks, keep this open."

An alarm chimed. Not an attack. A dockside incident flag. Mara frowned and pulled it up.

"Small fire in 2-Kappa," she said. "Two injuries. One fatality."

"Name," Seris said.

Mara scanned. The answer took longer than it should have. Her voice softened. "Kell."

Seris did not speak. She watched a tug nose a barge into its slot with infinite patience. After a moment she set her jaw.

"Send a team," she said. "Find who lit that fire and bring me their names. When you write the notice, say Kell died in dock service and that we owe him our lives. You can leave the rest between us and the Shards."

Mara nodded and moved. The bridge settled into the quiet of competent work. Resolve curved into her altered loop.

Seris sat, opened her log, and began to write. Not a speech. Not poetry. The kind of words that other wardens could stand on when the floor under them started to crack.

She wrote the seals and the shells. She wrote Pryce's smile and Rallis's knives. She wrote the way the crowd changed when a show ended and a fight began. She wrote that a corridor had moved three spans to the left and that there was air there for anyone who needed it.

She did not write the part where her oath had begun to come apart in her hands. She suspected that part would show on its own.

Chapter 17 – Drax's Ambition

Varak's night had the color of a forge. Smoke drifted low across the citadel like torn banners, and the vents below breathed a steady glow that pulsed against the cliff walls. In the Hall of Iron, drums beat a slow pattern that matched the rise and fall of the furnaces. War-standards hung from ribbed beams, each one stitched with the names of shards taken and rivals broken.

Drax Korren stood at the balcony rail with his gauntlet off, palm open to the heat. The skin there had thickened into a second armor long ago. He liked to feel the burn before he spoke to men. It reminded him what power costs, and what it gives back.

The doors boomed. A runner skidded to one knee on the iron tiles and held up a wrapped bundle no bigger than a skull.

"From the Rift-born flotilla, Lord Warlord. A witness shard. The Maw stirred."

Drax took the bundle and unwrapped wire and cloth. Inside lay a piece of crystal as black as quenched iron, crooked and heavy in the hand. It faintly pulsed under his thumb, a sick little heartbeat that made the air feel thinner.

He closed his fist around it. Pain lanced his palm and ran up his arm. He smiled.

"Summon the guild captains," he said. "Light the demonstration hall."

The runner sprinted away.

Drax turned the shard and studied the hairline veins dimming and brightening like a breath. He had seen shards glow before. Pilgrim toys. Echo baubles. This was not that. This remembered hunger. He slipped it into a shielded clutch on his belt and walked the long stair to the hall.

The demonstration chamber was a ring of iron galleries around a pit where a gimbal mounted the Warlord's private treasure. Engineers called it a fragment. Priests called it a sin. Drax called it a lever. It floated in its cradle, a bronze fist's worth of something that was not stone and not machine, crossed with pale lines that crawled like frost over river ice.

Guild captains filed in, soot still on their faces, armor unbuckled at the collar. Officers followed, the best of Varak's steel. Above them, merchant princes took their boxes, perfume and fear thick in the air. When the drums stilled, the room held its breath.

Drax walked to the railing. "A Maw woke," he said. "Not fully. Not yet. The clans howled and fled. A priestess bent it back to sleep. A smuggler held a map that pointed deeper. The Obsidian turned their heads like hounds. Meridian turned theirs away like cowards who know the smell of their own rot. The Belt just grew teeth. So will we."

He lifted his hand. The engineers at the console flinched, then obeyed. The fragment in the gimbal thrummed. The light in its veins brightened from moon to blade. The air took on weight. Men leaned forward without meaning to. A metal bust in the pit, a Forge-State eagle cast in solid steel, set to test the field, began to sag around the edges.

"Measure," Drax said.

"Local vector increased by two. Field integrity stable. No sign of sympathetic coupling with the mount," murmured the chief engineer, a thin woman with weld scars on both wrists.

"Three," Drax said.

The engineer swallowed and adjusted the rings. The fragment sang, not a sound, a pressure. The eagle's beak bent to a curve that no sculptor had intended. Rivets in the floor pinged like insects trapped in glass.

"Four," Drax said.

The engineer hesitated. He did not repeat himself. She turned the ring.

The field grew heavy. No one moved. The steel bust flattened as if pressed by a giant hand. In the galleries, a merchant prince clutched the rail with white knuckles and started to pray, remembered Drax's law against that in this hall, and fell silent.

Drax raised two fingers. The engineer cut power cleanly. The field vanished. Men exhaled in a ragged chorus.

He reached for the clutch at his belt and held up the black shard raised from the Maw. "This is a splinter of what sleeps in dead stone. It is not a god. It is not a friend. It is a tool for those with the will to lay their hands on it."

He dropped the shard into a lead-lined tray. The sound it made when it struck was small. The officers leaned forward as one.

"Rovik," Drax said.

A broad man with a collar of chain stepped out from the captain's line. "Lord."

"You take Iron Banner and Cutthroat. You will lift within the hour. You will hunt a small ship, Rift-born make, hull scarred, captain answers to Kael Veyra. He travels with an Echo named Liora. You bring me the map they carry. The priestess breathes when she arrives. I want to hear her sing to stone. The smuggler breathes if he is quiet."

Rovik nodded once. "Vectors, Lord."

"Cold trails run from the Maw toward the Drift's inner throat." Drax tapped a table and a map fan grew: fragments, bridge lanes, ghost routes that scouts had guessed and pirates had made. He set three bright pieces on the fan like bones on a drumhead. "They will need fuel, and air, and luck. Set nets along the routes that feed those things."

He looked up to the merchant boxes. "Dyers. Smelters. Load lancers and cutters. You will leave your sons behind to count coin. Today, you are citizens again."

There was a murmur, half protest and half pride. He let it run for a heartbeat, then sharpened his voice.

"I will take tariffs in blood if I must. I prefer steel. Put your ships under captains who can land without scraping the hull. If you cannot find such men, I will find them for you."

The murmur died clean.

A messenger with council blue edging his tabard stood at the doorway, trying to make himself small and failing. Drax beckoned. The man approached with a careful bow.

"From our friends at the Accord," the messenger said, passing a sealed slip. "They say a High Warden has gone off script. Patrol windows are shifting. A sealed operation compromised."

Drax cracked the seal with his thumb. The note inside was brief, a line of coordinates and a time, a promise that a bridge lane would be less watched than it should be. He felt the old twist of contempt. The Accord sold words about order to the weak and routes to the strong. He had never expected more.

"Tell your master the Accord does not need to move," Drax said. "Only to hold still where I need the floor empty. If they can manage that trick, I will remember it when I write the new laws."

The messenger bowed again and retreated in relief.

Drax turned to the engineers. "Pack the fragment. Field crew Alpha travels with Iron Banner. I want demonstration capacity at every forward platform. If a clan calls my bluff, you will show them why their bones sing in the night."

The chief engineer cleared her throat. "Lord, the fragment couples with mass. We can increase local vector, yes, we can warp fields in a radius, yes, but each surge fatigues the mount. There is a limit."

Drax stepped down into the pit and picked up the deformed eagle by the wing. The metal was warm and heavy. He squeezed with his flesh hand until it dented. He let it drop.

"Everything has a limit," he said. "Resolve is the art of pretending you do not."

He reached for his gauntlet and fastened it with a twist. The lock clicked like a door closing.

"Zira," he called.

A woman in a coat of scale and smoke, long knives at her hips, stepped from the shadow at a pillar. Her smile was neat and tired.

"My Lord Warlord."

"You will take a speaking ship to Jorren's fleet. Bring gifts for his quartermasters and coins for his cowards. Tell him I am coming behind with steel and flame. Tell him a smuggler he hates carries my prize. Watch which way his head turns when you speak the name Kael. Then tell me where to put the knife."

Zira's smile did not change. "And if he takes the coin and pretends not to remember the knife exists."

"Then you remind him," Drax said.

She bowed and was gone, thin as smoke.

The galleries had warmed with bodies and breath. The hall smelled like a city of ovens. Drax knew how to speak to men when the air was like this. He folded his hands behind his back and let his voice travel the iron.

"Listen. Meridian will send letters. The Obsidian will send quiet men with glass faces. The Riftborn will sing of old ghosts. None of them will build a bridge that holds. We will. We can cut gravity, shape tide, bend lanes to our will. Fear is a tool like heat, no more wicked than a hammer. Use it, and it makes shape. Be used by it, and it burns you hollow."

He let his eyes find the merchant princes. They stood straighter without meaning to. Good. He let his gaze pass to the captains. They looked at the fragment and then at him. Better.

"When the Belt broke, we learned what happens when the sky stops being one piece. The first law is simple. Pieces starve. United things eat. I intend to feed my people. The map these two carry is a knife that can cut all our throats or open a path through our hunger. I will hold the haft."

He lifted his hand. "Forge tempo. Two shifts, no sleep between. Dock crews on double rations. Signal to all vent-cities. Muster. The fleet lifts in six hours."

He left them with their orders and climbed the stairs. His private corridor ran along the cliff face, windows set close, stone kept bare. He preferred to walk without witnesses between decisions. The passage opened into a smaller room where a single brazier burned low and a slab of basalt served as a table. A boy waited there, freckled, no more than fourteen, a runner with a knife and a face too young for the worry in it.

"What is it," Drax said, softer without meaning to be.

The boy swallowed. "My mother says I should tell you truth. They say you ask for truth. They say you keep men who speak it."

"Speak," Drax said.

"Some in the forges say the shard in the gimbal is a curse. They say it sings wrong. My mother says a man's tool does not sing. The hand sings. She says if you hear a song, it is your own heart and you should not fear it."

Drax stood very still. He remembered a roof of tin over a bed near a vent, the sound of rain made of ash, a hand on his hair when he was smaller than this boy. He forced the memory back into the iron box where he kept such things.

"Tell your mother she is right," he said. "Tell her to keep her boys out of demonstration halls. Tell her she will have work when the guild closes its fists. I am not done building."

The boy's shoulders unhooked. He nodded and fled.

Drax stood by the window until the drums below found a faster beat. He could see the lifts from here. Crates rising on cables. Armor being checked by men who would not see their homes again for months. Torches moving across the yards like fireflies that had learned discipline.

He took the Maw shard from his belt and held it to the glass. The pulse had slowed since he wrapped it, as if Varak's heat had lulled it. He breathed on it. The light quickened.

"Wake if you must," he said to the shard and to the world that had made it. "Do it on my timetable."

Rovik's voice came from the doorway, crisp and ready. "Lord. Iron Banner reports green. Cutthroat is fueling. The guild has delivered six lancers and three cutters. The merchants sent sons with them. Names worth reading."

"Good," Drax said. "Make their names worth remembering."

He slid the shard back into its clutch. "Bring me Kael Veyra alive if you can. Bring me the priestess alive even if you cannot bring anyone else. Bring me the map above all things. If you must choose who breathes and who does not, choose the map. I will forgive the rest."

Rovik saluted with the old clenched fist. "By iron and ash."

Drax returned it. "By iron and ash."

The horn towers brayed. Deep notes rolled through the citadel, the sound that meant fleets were rising. Drax walked to the outer balcony and watched engines lift from their cradles like sunrise made of metal. The wind that rose with them smelled of oil and hot glass and the inside of a furnace. He filled his lungs and felt strong.

In the smoke above the far ridge a small black shape hung for a breath and then slid away, silent and patient. Drax did not see it, and if he had, he would have called it a trick of heat. The Obsidian Order had already arrived, uninvited as always, content to gather what his noise would shake loose.

The Warlord raised his gauntlet as if he could hold the rising ships in his palm. In the gesture was no magic. Only claim. He lowered his hand and turned to where the maps waited in their light.

"Bring me the Belt," he said, to the officers and the engineers and to the shard in his pocket. "I will hammer it into one piece."

Chapter 18 – A Fragile Alliance

The Riftborn flotilla moored inside a broken ring-station, its skeletal girders wrapped around the fragment like the ribs of some ancient beast. Fires burned in braziers along the hangar decks. The air was thick with smoke and sweat, and the smell of oil clung to every surface.

Kael stood near the *Wraith's Fortune*, his wrists still raw from manacles. He could feel the eyes on him—Riftborn warriors sharpening blades, elders watching from the shadows, children whispering about the smuggler who had lived through the fire. Some looked at him with contempt. Others with something closer to curiosity.

They didn't look at him for long. Their gazes turned to Liora.

She moved among them as if the smoke parted for her. The burns on her palms were bound with cloth, but her presence had only grown since the Maw. The fire that had bent to her hands still lived in their minds. Warriors who would have spat at an Echo yesterday now inclined their heads when she passed. Elders touched their talismans. Even the children followed her steps like a tide.

Kael hated how fragile that reverence felt. It could turn to fear in a heartbeat, and fear always sharpened into knives.

Jorren knew it too.

The Riftborn war-captain stood at the center of the hangar with his scarred face lit by the brazier glow. His men gathered around him, armor clattering, weapons slung across backs and hips. His implant eye whirred as it scanned the crowd, measuring loyalties like weights on a scale.

When Liora and Kael approached, the noise dimmed.

Jorren's voice carried like a hammer strike. "You all saw it. You all felt it. The Maw woke. It was our raid, our blood, our fire that kept it from tearing the Shard apart. And yet—" His gaze locked on Liora. "It was not our song that silenced it. It was hers."

A ripple passed through the gathered clans. Some nodded. Others scowled.

Jorren lifted a hand. "The Riftborn are strong because we do not kneel. We do not follow priests, or wardens, or Meridian cowards. We follow strength. That is our law."

He turned his gaze on Kael, and the contempt there was sharp enough to cut. "And what of him? The traitor who sold our blood to Meridian, who ran while brothers burned? Will we follow him too? Will we forget the fire that ate our kin?"

The roar of anger that followed made Kael's gut twist. He clenched his fists, ready for a fight he knew he could not win.

But Liora stepped forward.

Her voice was calm, but it carried like water over stone. "You are right. Kael Veyra is no Riftborn. He carries blood on his hands. He carries shame. But the Shards themselves spared him. You all saw it in the fire. He was judged, and the fire passed him by. You would spit on their judgment?"

The crowd shifted uneasily.

Jorren's jaw tightened. "Words. Pretty words. The clans need iron, not whispers."

"Then look at your iron," Liora said. She raised her bound hands. "Your raids bring food for a day, fuel for a week. But the Shards are stirring. You all felt it in the Maw. The next time, it will not be one hollow. It will be all of them. Who among you will silence that? Who among you can bend fire, or still a broken heart of stone?"

Silence.

Kael looked at the faces around him. Hard men and women, scarred by a life of hunger and blood. They wanted to laugh, to jeer, but they could not deny what they had seen with their own eyes.

An elder with hair like ash spoke first. "The priestess speaks truth. I saw the fire bend. I saw the Maw falter. We cannot spit on a sign."

Others muttered agreement.

Jorren's eye burned red. "You would give her your loyalty? To a stranger who sings to ghosts?"

A younger captain barked from the edge of the crowd. "Better ghosts than your grudges, Jorren. How long will you choke us with the past?"

The murmur grew louder. Some shouted for Liora. Others for Jorren.

Kael felt the tension thicken, a storm building in the smoke. If it broke here, in this hangar, blood would drown them all.

He stepped forward, heart hammering.

"I'm not asking for loyalty," he said, loud enough to cut through the noise. "I wouldn't give it if I were you. I've earned your hate. Fine. Keep it. But listen to her. Because she's right—this isn't about raids anymore. The Shards are waking. You think Meridian will save you? You think Drax will? They'll bleed you dry and leave your bones for the void. The only chance you have is her. The only chance we all have is her."

The silence that followed was heavier than any roar.

Jorren's face was carved stone. He stepped close, close enough that Kael could smell the oil on his armor. "You dare speak as if you are Riftborn again."

Kael didn't flinch. "No. I speak as someone who knows what it means to run. I won't do it this time."

For a heartbeat, Kael thought Jorren would kill him then and there.

But Jorren only snarled, turned, and raised his blade high.

"Then hear it. Some of you will follow her. Some of you will stay with me. We will not cut each other's throats today, but this alliance is no chain. It holds only as long as it must. The first sign of weakness, and I will break it myself."

The clans roared, half in agreement, half in defiance.

Kael let out a breath he hadn't realized he was holding. Liora's hand brushed his arm. Her eyes were steady, but he could see the wear in them.

A fragile alliance had been forged. Fragile enough to break at the first strain. But for now, it was enough.

Chapter 19 – The Silent Assassin

The *Wraith's Fortune* slept in the cradle of the broken ring-station. The Riftborn fires burned low now, sending thin plumes of smoke into the dark. Most of the clans had sunk into their cups or their bedrolls, singing rough songs until voices cracked. The hangar felt almost peaceful. Almost.

Kael lay on his bunk aboard the *Fortune*, staring at the ceiling plate that still bore scorch marks from the Maw. His body ached from too many days of running, fighting, and nearly dying. His mind wouldn't let him rest. Every time he closed his eyes, he saw the fire folding around Liora's hands, or Jorren's sneer as the clans split, or Drax's fleets rising like a steel tide.

He reached into his jacket and touched the capsule. The relic pulsed faintly, a heartbeat against his palm. He wanted to throw it out the airlock. He wanted to chain it to the deck. He wanted to sell it, drink until the universe went quiet, and forget. But he couldn't let go.

A sound broke his thoughts.

Not the groan of metal or the distant laughter of Riftborn. A whisper. A scrape. Something soft where nothing should move.

Kael sat up, hand sliding toward the pistol on his belt. The sound came again, from the corridor outside his cabin.

He stood slowly, careful not to make the deck creak. The pistol felt heavy but right in his grip. He eased the hatch open.

The corridor was dark. Too dark. The auxiliary lamps that should have lit a faint glow were dead.

Kael's gut tightened. He had lived long enough to know when someone had killed the light on purpose.

He moved down the hall, slow, every step measured. His ears strained for sound. For a moment there was nothing. Then—air moving, fast.

A shadow cut across him. Too fast. He ducked, twisted, fired. The blast lit the corridor in harsh white. Nothing. No body. No sound. Only a faint ripple, like water disturbed.

Kael swore under his breath.

A whisper came from behind him. Cold. Low. "Smuggler."

He spun, firing again. The blast seared into the wall. Empty.

The voice came again, closer now. "The Shards do not sing for you. They never did."

Kael's heart pounded. His palms were slick. He had faced soldiers, pirates, bounty hunters. He had never felt this. Not fear of dying, but fear of being erased.

Then he saw it.

A mask, pale and smooth, hovering in the dark. No eyes. No mouth. Just a blank face. The Assassin.

Kael raised his pistol. The figure moved with impossible speed. A blade flashed. The pistol spun from Kael's hand, clattering against the bulkhead.

The Assassin didn't strike to kill. Not yet. The blade rested at Kael's throat. Cold. Perfectly steady.

"You carry noise," the voice whispered. "Noise wakes memory. The Order demands silence."

The blade pressed closer. Kael's breath caught.

Then a light flared at the end of the corridor. A hum filled the air. Liora's staff.

The Assassin turned its mask.

Liora stood barefoot, robes loose from sleep, her staff glowing faintly in her hands. Her eyes were bright, sharp. "He lives," she said. Her voice rang clear, like a bell in still air. "Or I burn your silence to ash."

The Assassin's head tilted. "Echo."

Liora lifted the staff. The hum deepened. The air shivered. Kael felt it in his bones, a vibration that wanted to break the world apart.

The Assassin moved. Too fast. The blade flicked, drawing a line of blood across Kael's neck, then darted for Liora.

She struck the deck with her staff. The hum exploded outward. The corridor shook. Light burst from the staff's crystal, raw resonance that turned the metal walls into singing plates.

The Assassin faltered. Its blade wavered. For the first time, it seemed to slow.

Liora pressed harder. The glow wrapped her hands, her arms, her whole body trembling with the strain. Blood welled at her nose. Her lips trembled with words Kael couldn't hear.

The Assassin staggered back, mask tilting as if listening to something beyond them both. Its voice was colder now. "Not silence. Not yet. But soon."

Then it was gone. One breath it was there. The next it melted into the dark, leaving only the faint echo of its whisper.

The light from Liora's staff faded. She swayed, her knees buckling.

Kael caught her before she fell. Her skin was burning hot, her breath shallow.

"Idiot," he muttered, voice rough. "You burned yourself out."

Her eyes fluttered open. She managed a faint smile. "You're welcome."

Kael held her tight. His own hands shook, though he'd never admit it. The blood at his throat was warm. The capsule still pulsed in his pocket, steady as ever, as if none of it had happened.

But Kael knew.

The Assassin had found them. And it would not stop until the Shards were silent again.

Chapter 20 – The Rift Splits

The Riftborn called it the Council of Chains. They gathered in the old ring-station's hollow spine, beneath broken girders strung with banners of bone and iron. Fires burned in pits cut into the deck, the smoke venting through cracks in the walls. Warriors beat drums made from fuel drums, the sound heavy as heartbeats.

Kael stood at the edge of the circle with his back to the *Wraith's Fortune*. Every eye seemed to find him no matter how still he stood. His neck still ached where the Assassin's blade had grazed him. He could still hear that whisper in the dark.

Liora sat beside him, pale but upright. Her hands were bandaged from the resonance she had unleashed. Her staff leaned against her shoulder, the crystal faintly pulsing with her own heartbeat. She said nothing, but her presence was louder than any speech. The Riftborn eyes that lingered on Kael slid quickly past to her.

Jorren stood in the center, scarred face lit by the firepits. His implant eye whirred as it studied the clans arrayed before him. Captains and elders lined the circle, armor scarred, tattoos stark in the smoke. Behind them, warriors filled the shadows, restless, muttering.

"You all saw it," Jorren growled. "The Maw. The fire. The priestess who bent it, and the smuggler who walked away from judgment. Now you see the truth: Obsidian assassins hunt them. Forge-States raise fleets. Meridian whispers rot from its own council. And we—" He pounded his chest, the sound echoing. "We are asked to follow them."

The crowd roared in anger, then split in shouts.

"She is chosen by the Shards!" one elder called.

"She is a liar!" another spat.

"He carries the map!"

"He carries betrayal!"

The noise grew into a storm, clans shouting across the fire. Kael felt the tension coil in his gut. This wasn't a council. It was a tinderbox waiting for a spark.

Liora rose. She lifted her staff, the glow rising with it. The noise dimmed. Not silence, but enough.

Her voice rang clear. "You all know what hunts us. You saw the Maw stir. You felt its hunger. The Shards are not dead stone. They are waking. If we do not act together, we will all burn—Riftborn, Forge-State, Meridian alike. You can fight each other until your blood paints the fragments, but the Shards will not care. Only together do we stand a chance."

A murmur rippled through the crowd.

One captain sneered. "Together under you, priestess?"

"Not under me," Liora said. "With me. With Kael. With anyone who will face what comes. The Shards spared him. They answered me. That is not chance. That is a path."

Kael swallowed hard, hating how every eye turned to him. He forced himself to speak. "You don't have to like me. Hell, I don't like me. But I won't run this time. If you want to call me cursed, fine. Call me cursed. Just don't ignore what's coming."

The silence that followed stretched taut.

Then an elder with a crown of wires in her braids rose. "I have seen Echoes in three generations. None bent fire. None broke a Maw's heart. I will follow the priestess."

Another elder slammed his spear to the deck. "We are Riftborn. We do not bow to outside blood. I stay with Jorren."

The circle fractured. Shouts rose again. Warriors banged weapons against armor, sparks flying. Some cried Liora's name. Others roared Jorren's. The noise was a storm now, a storm tearing itself apart.

Jorren's implant eye burned red. He raised his blade high. "Enough! Let the clans split. Those who follow me, prepare for war. Those who follow her, bleed in silence. But know this—when you fall, I will not carry your bones."

The hangar erupted. Clans pulled apart, some gathering at Jorren's side, others drifting toward Kael and Liora. Weapons clattered. Oaths were shouted. The Riftborn were no longer one.

Kael's stomach sank. They had won some allies, but at the cost of unity.

Liora lowered her staff, her eyes weary but steady. "It was always going to break," she said softly. "Better it break now, before the true fire comes."

Kael looked at the faces around them—grim, scarred, but willing. A fragile band of allies.

But across the circle, Jorren's gaze locked on him with pure hatred. And Kael knew the Riftborn civil war had begun.

Chapter 21 – Into the Hidden Path

The capsule woke them before dawnshift.

Kael had been half-asleep on the *Fortune's* deck, back against a bulkhead, when the relic pulsed through his jacket. He jerked upright, cursing softly. The glow had grown sharper, no longer the faint heartbeat he had learned to dread. Now it cast thin lines of light across the deck, bleeding through the fabric like veins of fire.

Liora stirred from her meditation. She didn't ask what had happened. Her eyes found the glow at once. "It's ready," she said, her voice hushed.

Kael frowned. "Ready for what?"

Before Liora could answer, Resolve slipped into the ring-station's berth with silent thrusters. Meridian steel among Riftborn bone. The clans bristled, weapons rising, but Seris Thane walked down the cutter's ramp without hesitation. Her cloak was short, her pistol at her hip, her presence unflinching.

She ignored the Riftborn snarls and walked straight to Kael and Liora.

"You're about to leave," she said, calm as if remarking on the weather.

Kael's hand brushed his pistol. "How do you know that?"

Seris' eyes dropped to the capsule, its glow plain now in the gloom. "Because Meridian paid in blood to bury that light. I just dug up the grave."

Jorren's voice cut across the hangar. "Warden." His scarred face was twisted in a sneer. "Come to chain us for your Accord? Or to beg for scraps?"

Seris didn't so much as glance at him. "I'm here because I know what hunts you. Forge-State fleets are moving. The Obsidian is already in your shadow. If you follow that light without someone to watch your flank, you won't live to see where it leads."

Liora rose, staff in hand. "Then walk with us."

Jorren barked a laugh. "You would let a Meridian leash you? You are more of a fool than I thought."

The clans muttered. Some agreed. Others watched with wary silence.

Kael pushed to his feet, jaw tight. "Listen. None of us like each other. That's fine. But the capsule doesn't care. The Shards don't care. They're waking, and if we waste time pissing on old grudges, we're all dead."

Seris' eyes met his, cool and steady. "Then let's move."

The *Wraith's Fortune* slipped from the ring-station, Resolve falling into escort above and behind her. A handful of Riftborn ships joined them—those who had chosen Liora's path. The rest stayed with Jorren, their lights flaring in the dark like angry stars.

Inside the cockpit, Kael watched the capsule hover above the console. Its lines of light stretched forward, weaving a map into the void. Not a lane. Not a chart anyone sane would trust. But a path, nonetheless.

"Where does it go?" he asked.

Liora's gaze never left the glow. "Deeper than the Maw. Into a hidden corridor. A place even the Shards themselves forgot."

"That sounds comforting," Kael muttered.

Seris stood behind them, arms folded, her presence grounding the small cabin. "If Meridian tried to bury this, it means they feared it more than they feared Drax. That alone tells me it's worth reaching first."

The capsule pulsed. The *Fortune*'s sensors flickered. On the scopes, Kael saw only static, then a faint shimmer, like heat over stone. Beyond it, blackness deeper than night.

"That's it?" he asked. "Doesn't look like much."

Liora's hand brushed his arm. "Step through."

Kael swore under his breath, tightened his grip on the throttle, and pushed.

The void folded.

The cockpit stretched, then snapped back. For a moment Kael's vision blurred, and his stomach flipped as if the universe had turned inside out. Then the stars were gone.

The *Fortune* drifted in silence. Outside stretched a corridor of broken crystal walls, jagged and immense, glowing faintly with veins of pale light. The space between them was narrow—too narrow for anything larger than a cutter. The air felt thick even inside the cabin, as though the corridor itself pressed against them.

Kael let out a low breath. "Well. We're not dead. Yet."

Seris leaned closer to the viewport. "These walls... they're not natural. They've been cut."

"By who?" Kael asked.

"Not who," Liora said softly. "What."

Kael glanced at her. "You're not going to like, collapse again, are you?"

Her lips twitched faintly. "Not if you keep flying straight."

The capsule pulsed again, pointing deeper. The corridor wound on, the crystal walls humming faintly like strings under a bow. Shadows moved in the glow—shapes that might have been wrecks, or echoes of something older.

Kael swallowed hard, forcing his grip to stay steady on the controls. "Whatever's at the end of this path, it better be worth it."

No one answered.

Because all three of them knew the truth.

It would not be worth it.

It would be worse.

ACT III – The Broken Sky

Chapter 22 – Storm over Meridian

Meridian Prime shimmered above the bridge like a jewel built on glass. Its towers rose in rings, silver spines webbed together by arc-light bridges, every surface polished until the world below was a mirror of its own pride. To the merchants and guild leaders who lived within its walls, it was a symbol of order. To Seris Thane, watching from the viewport of her cutter Resolve, it looked more like a mask.

Docking clearance came with too much ceremony. Three patrol ships escorted her in, their lights glaring, their engines angled so every passerby could see the show. As Resolve eased into its berth, a delegation was already waiting: Councilor Venn in his pristine robes, guards in gilded armor, aides clutching slates. The image was crafted, painted, as false as the reports Seris carried in her satchel.

She walked down the gangway without bowing, cloak folded back to leave her pistol visible. Her boots rang sharp against the polished deck. The crowd parted uneasily at her pace, as if afraid she might draw the weapon simply to prove she could.

"High Warden," Venn said, smiling like a man who had practiced it in a mirror. "Welcome back to Prime. I trust your patrol was uneventful."

Seris stopped two steps from him. "One patrol cutter and eight wardens impounded weapons shipments moving under your seals. Relief crates stuffed with Forge-State munitions. If that is your definition of uneventful, Councilor, I suggest you buy a new lexicon."

The smile faltered. For the briefest flicker of a heartbeat, anger showed. Then it was smoothed away again. "You must understand—there are complexities to governance. Supply chains, security arrangements. Sometimes appearances—"

"Appearances kill people," Seris said flatly. "I do not enforce appearances. I enforce law."

The guards shifted uneasily. Whispers ran through the aides. Venn inclined his head with false grace. "Then by all means, High Warden, you may present your evidence to the full Council. They will be most eager to hear it."

The Council chamber was a circle of glass and steel suspended high above the city. Beneath the transparent floor, the towers glittered, and the bridges below were threads of light. The councillors sat in their high-backed chairs, robes layered and marked with guild crests. At the center, a dais waited.

Seris laid the satchel on the dais, opened it, and placed one of the powder-blue shells in the center of the glass. Gasps rippled around the chamber.

"Found in Anchor Twelve relief," Seris said. Her voice carried, sharp and clear. "Signed under Councilor Venn's authorizations. Routed through your patrol edits. I have chain of custody logs from Port Ring Three. I have recordings of your security inspector ordering me to stand down. I have names, signatures, times. If any one of you wishes to deny this, I suggest you do it while I am still in the room."

The chamber erupted in voices. Some angry, some shocked, some deliberately confused. Hands slapped the table. Accusations flew.

One councillor, Hale, leaned forward, his voice oily but smooth. "High Warden Thane, even if your accusations are true, do you understand what you risk? Stability is fragile. The Riftborn grow restless. The Forge-States arm for war. If the people see weakness in us, if they believe the Council compromised, the Accord itself could fracture."

Seris met his gaze without blinking. "Then perhaps it deserves to fracture."

The room went still.

Venn rose, face red with contained fury. "You overstep, Thane. You forget your place. You are a warden of the bridge. You are not a councillor. You are not a voice. You are a sword. And when a sword cuts its own hand, it must be broken."

Two guards stepped forward. The chamber expected Seris to resist. Instead she placed her hands calmly on the dais. Her voice was steady.

"If you mean to silence me, you will have to do it in the open. In front of your peers. In front of your people. The proof is here. The shells are here. Even if you strike me down, the stain is on your robes."

For a moment, she thought Venn would order it anyway. His jaw clenched. His eyes flicked to the guards. But then he saw the councillors watching him, weighing him, and he sat back down.

"Remove her," he spat. "Until the Council decides what to do with a traitor."

The guards gripped Seris' arms. She did not struggle.

They held her in a tower cell that overlooked the glittering sprawl of Meridian Prime. From here, the city looked clean. The corruption beneath its bridges was invisible. That was always the way of masks.

Mara Pell slipped through the door at duskshift, face pale, hands quick. She carried no uniform now, only the cloak of a civilian.

"High Warden," she whispered.

Seris allowed herself a small smile. "Not anymore."

"You have allies," Mara said. "Quiet ones. Dock guilds, some wardens who still remember their oaths. They will move if you ask. But it will mean open defiance. No more shadows."

Seris looked out at the city. Lights shimmered on the bridges like false stars. She thought of the Riftborn clans tearing themselves apart. She thought of the Forge-State fleets rising. She thought of Kael and Liora vanishing into a hidden path where no map should lead.

Her voice was low but steady. "Then we will not hide. If the Council calls me traitor, I will wear the name. But I will keep the bridge open. Whatever else breaks, that law holds."

Mara's eyes glistened. She clasped Seris' hand briefly, then turned to prepare.

Seris stood at the window as the city glittered below. Storms gathered on the horizon. She knew when it broke, Meridian would never look the same again.

And she no longer cared.

Chapter 23 – Drax's Siege

The Forge-State fleets rose like a stormfront of iron and fire.

From the viewport of the *Iron Banner*, Captain Rovik watched the war machines ignite the night. Lines of warships stretched across the fragment horizon, their engines burning gold and red, their hulls scarred with the weldmarks of a hundred reforgings. Lancers, cutters, troop-carriers — an armada born in the firepits of Varak, each one carrying the stamp of Drax Korren's will.

And at the heart of it, the Warlord's flagship, *Ashfang*. A beast of a ship, built from the bones of three battleships, welded together into a silhouette too ugly and too vast to mistake. Its prow carried a mounted fragment, the same bronze fist Drax had demonstrated in the Hall of Iron. Even through the hull, Rovik could feel the field humming in his teeth.

"Signal from *Ashfang*," his comms officer said. "Lord Warlord speaks to all fleets."

The channel opened with a low growl, then Drax's voice, iron and smoke.

"Brothers. Sisters. Forged blood. Today the clans will remember who holds the hammer. The Riftborn defy me. They scatter like sparks in the dark. I will stamp them into one fire. They will learn that pieces starve and united things eat. Strike the Riftborn strongholds. Leave their songs in ash. But bring me Kael Veyra alive. Bring me the priestess whole. Above all, bring me the map."

The fleet answered with a roar of engines, a chorus of horns, a thunder that carried across the void.

The Riftborn bastion at Shardfall was little more than a jagged ring of crystal, scarred by centuries of raids and patched with rusting plates. They had no fleets like Forge-State, only swarms of skiffs, raiders, and old freighters armed with guns stripped from wrecks. But they had fury, and fury burned hotter than fuel.

Kael stood on the *Wraith's Fortune's* deck as alarms screamed. Riftborn ships surged from the station like hornets from a nest, engines howling, shields sparking.

Jorren's voice cut across the channel, harsh and fierce. "To arms! Steel to steel! Show the Forge-States our bones do not bend!"

Kael swore under his breath. "Bones don't bend, but they break just fine."

Liora stood beside him, her staff braced against the deck. Her face was pale, her body still weakened from the fight with the Assassin, but her eyes blazed with a fire stronger than her frame. "We cannot hold them with steel alone."

"What do you want me to do?" Kael snapped. "Spit at them? These are fleets, Liora. Armies."

Her voice was steady. "Not spit. Memory." She placed her hand on the capsule where it hovered above the console. The glow sharpened, its lines weaving a map across the void. "The Shards remember paths they have hidden. If I can reach them, I can show the Riftborn a way to strike where the Forge is blind."

Kael hesitated, then nodded. He tightened his grip on the throttle. "All right. Let's remind them."

The first clash came like thunder. Forge-State lancers cut through Riftborn skiffs with beams of molten light, splitting ships into slag. Riftborn swarms darted through the chaos, slashing with torpedoes, ramming when their ammo ran dry. The void filled with fire, debris, and bodies spinning silently in the dark.

Jorren led from the front in his warship, *Bloodsong*, ramming through a Forge-State cutter, boarding with axes and blades. His voice rang over open comms, savage, fearless. "We bleed, but we bleed with purpose! Hold!"

On the *Ashfang*, Drax stood on the command dais, gauntlet raised. "Bring the fragment field online."

The mounted shard in the prow flared. The air seemed to thicken across the void. Riftborn ships staggered, their engines groaning, their trajectories skewed. The field dragged them like toys in a child's hand. One skiff buckled under the pressure, hull plates folding inward.

Drax smiled grimly. "Show them what a hammer feels like."

The *Ashfang*'s guns roared.

Kael fought the controls, swearing as the *Fortune* lurched under the shard-field's weight. "This isn't flying. It's drowning!"

Liora's hands shook as she forced resonance through the capsule. The map flared brighter, showing cracks in the field's grip, small veins of open space. "There! Slide between the lines. The field cannot hold everything."

Kael gritted his teeth and angled the *Fortune* into the gap. The ship bucked, metal groaning, but broke through the weight into open dark. A Riftborn skiff followed, then another.

"Tell them," Kael snapped.

Liora opened the channel. Her voice rang through every Riftborn speaker. "Follow the light. Strike where the Forge cannot see. The Shards show you the cracks."

For a heartbeat, silence. Then Riftborn ships wheeled, darting through the hidden lines, slipping free of the shard-field's grip. They struck the

Forge flanks, their torpedoes tearing into engines, their boarding hooks sinking deep.

The battle roared anew.

But even with the hidden paths, the Forge fleets pressed harder. For every Riftborn ship that struck true, two more were burned. The *Bloodsong* was scarred, venting atmosphere from three decks. Jorren fought like a man possessed, but even his fury could not turn the tide forever.

On the *Ashfang*, Drax watched the Riftborn rally with cold amusement. "They fight like starving dogs. Good. A hammer makes no music if the iron does not scream."

Rovik approached, armor scorched. "Lord, they will not hold much longer."

Drax's gauntlet clenched. "Break their stronghold. Leave nothing standing. But mark the *Wraith's Fortune*. That ship is mine."

Kael's console lit red. Multiple locks. Too many. The *Fortune* shook as fire ripped across her shields.

"We can't hold here!" Kael shouted.

Liora's voice was thin but steady. "The path goes deeper. We must follow it."

Kael stared at her. "If we run, the Riftborn die."

"If we stay, everyone dies," Seris' voice cut in from Resolve, holding the flank with disciplined bursts of fire. Her calm tone carried iron. "Kael, Liora's right. The path is the only chance. Find what's at the end, and maybe this war isn't lost before it begins."

Kael's hands trembled on the controls. He looked at the battle—ships burning, Riftborn bleeding, Forge fleets pressing like a tide. He wanted to stay. He wanted to run. He wanted to do both.

Liora touched his arm. Her eyes were fierce. "Trust me."

For once, Kael did.

He threw the *Fortune* into the corridor of light. Resolve and a handful of Riftborn ships followed. Behind them, Shardfall burned.

Drax watched from the *Ashfang* as the *Fortune* vanished into the hidden path. His gauntlet clenched, not in frustration, but in satisfaction.

"Good," he murmured. "Run, little smuggler. Lead me to the heart."

Behind him, the fragment field pulsed. The Riftborn bastion cracked apart, fire spilling into the void. The siege had begun, and the Belt itself trembled with its echo.

Chapter 24 – Shadows at the Core

The hidden corridor narrowed until the void itself felt like a throat closing around them.

The *Wraith's Fortune* drifted between crystal walls that glowed faintly, veins of pale blue pulsing as though the Shard itself had a heartbeat. The hull groaned as if it disliked being here, as if the ship knew what Kael refused to say aloud: this place was wrong.

Kael hunched over the controls, jaw tight, eyes darting across failing readings. "Sensors are blind. Comms are junk. We're flying half by instinct, half by your glowing toy."

The capsule hovered above the console, its light spilling thin, weaving lines deeper into the corridor. Every so often the lines shivered, then reformed, as though the map itself was remembering where it wanted them to go.

Behind him, Seris stood silent, one hand resting on the bulkhead for balance. Even she seemed unnerved, her calm mask stretched thin by the weight of the place.

Liora sat cross-legged on the deck, staff across her knees, eyes closed. Her breathing was slow, steady, too deliberate to be natural. Sweat glistened on her brow.

"You're listening to it, aren't you?" Kael muttered.

Her eyes opened. They glowed faintly in the capsule's light. "It's not a voice. Not words. Just... impressions. Memory burned into stone."

Kael grunted. "Hope it's good memories. The last ones nearly killed us."

Seris moved closer to the viewport, gaze sharp. "Kael. Lights ahead."

He frowned, leaning forward. The glow at the corridor's end pulsed brighter, washing the crystal walls in a sickly shimmer. Wrecks floated there—dozens of them. Riftborn skiffs, Meridian cutters, even a Forge-

State lancer, all torn open, their hulls twisted into shapes that looked less like battle scars and more like they'd been melted, reshaped.

Kael swore under his breath. "Looks like the graveyard keeps itself tidy."

Liora rose slowly, her hand on the staff for balance. "These ships didn't just die. They were absorbed. The Shard remembers them. Holds them."

Seris' jaw tightened. "Then we keep moving. Slowly. Eyes open."

Kael eased the *Fortune* forward, threading between wrecks that hung like bones in a giant's throat. The capsule's light drew them onward, deeper, always deeper.

That was when the hum began.

Soft at first, barely audible, more a vibration than a sound. Then sharper, crawling into their teeth, their bones. Kael winced, shaking his head. "Tell me that's normal."

Liora's voice was barely more than a whisper. "No. That's not the Shard."

Seris drew her pistol, eyes scanning the shadows. "Then what is it?"

The answer came with a flicker of motion.

A mask appeared in the viewport. Smooth. Pale. Blank.

Kael's heart lurched. He yanked the controls. The *Fortune* spun sideways as a blade of light slashed past the hull, scoring a molten scar across its plating.

"The Assassin," he hissed.

The mask vanished into the wrecks, the hum fading with it.

Seris steadied herself, eyes narrowed. "How in the void did it follow us through the corridor?"

"Doesn't matter," Kael snapped, checking the readouts. "It's here."

Another flicker. Another slash. The *Fortune* shuddered, alarms blaring.

The capsule pulsed violently, its light scattering into frantic lines. Liora clutched her staff, her eyes wide. "It's not just following. It's guiding."

Kael blinked at her. "Guiding?"

"It knows this place. It knows the paths. It's trying to push us off them."

The *Fortune* bucked again as something struck the hull, hard enough to send Kael slamming into his harness. Sparks showered from the console.

Seris braced herself against the wall, pistol steady. "Then we hunt it. It stalks us in the dark, but it bleeds like anything else."

Kael shot her a look. "You sound awfully sure."

Seris' mouth twitched in something like a smile. "I've been waiting for something I could shoot that deserved it."

The hum swelled again. This time it wasn't one note but many, layered, discordant. The wrecks around them shifted, drifting closer, as though pulled by the same vibration.

Liora's voice was sharp. "It's using the echoes. Twisting the Shard's memory against us."

Kael's hands clenched the controls. "Great. It's not enough that it wants to kill us. Now the walls are helping."

The capsule flared suddenly, its light shooting straight down into the core of the corridor. A new line formed on the map, sharp and clear. A way forward.

Liora gasped, clutching her chest. "There. That's the true path. If we follow it, we can outrun the echo."

"And if we don't?" Kael asked.

The Assassin's mask flickered back into the viewport, close now, too close. The blade in its hand pulsed with stolen light.

Seris lifted her pistol. "Then we die here."

Kael slammed the throttle. The *Fortune* roared forward into the narrow vein of light. The walls shook, the wrecks scraped past, and the hum rose to a scream.

The Assassin's mask lingered for a heartbeat longer in the viewport, then vanished into the shadows.

But Kael knew it hadn't gone. It was waiting. Watching.

And at the end of this path, whatever waited would not be the Assassin's trap. It would be worse.

Chapter 25 – The Echo Bleeds

The *Wraith's Fortune* drifted into a cavern of crystal unlike any Kael had ever seen. The corridor spilled out into a vast hollow, its walls curving like the inside of a ribcage, veins of pale light crawling across them. The glow reflected on wrecks suspended in the air, some ancient, some fresh, all caught like flies in amber.

At the center of the cavern floated something that was not wreckage.

A sphere of crystal hung there, black veined with light, its surface pulsing in slow rhythm. Every pulse sent ripples through the hollow, a resonance that made the hull of the *Fortune* shiver. The capsule on the console flared in response, its own lines reaching toward the sphere as if drawn.

Liora gripped her staff with both hands, her body trembling. Her eyes were fixed on the sphere. "That's a shard-heart. But... no. It's more than that. It's bleeding."

Kael frowned. "Bleeding?"

"Resonance," she said through clenched teeth. "It's leaking. Memory, power, all spilling out at once. If it keeps going, the hollow will collapse—and everything inside with it."

Seris leaned forward, her pistol steady but useless against what hung before them. "Then close it. Seal it."

Liora shook her head. "It's not that simple. The heart is tangled. Too many echoes feeding into it, too many paths overlapping. I'll need to thread them back into place."

Kael's gut twisted. "That sounds like a suicide sentence."

Her eyes met his, fierce and steady. "It's the only way."

Before Kael could protest, the capsule pulsed harder, almost frantic. The *Fortune's* lights flickered. A low hum filled the cabin, deepening until Kael felt his teeth ache.

Then the hum split into voices.

Whispers, hundreds of them, overlapping, some too faint to hear, others sharp and cruel. Kael pressed his palms to his ears, but the voices weren't in his ears. They were in his bones.

"You left them," one hissed. "You ran while brothers burned."

Kael's chest clenched. He knew that voice. He'd heard it on the day he fled Jorren's fleet, the day he bought his freedom with blood.

"Your oath is ash," another whispered. It was Sira's voice, though she wasn't here.

Kael staggered, his vision blurring. He saw shadows moving in the cabin—faces of those he had lost, those he had failed.

Seris swore softly, staggering against the bulkhead. Her eyes widened as she saw the faces of her own wardens, men and women she had buried, staring at her through the glass.

The shard-heart was bleeding their memories into the air.

Liora alone stood unmoved, though her body shook with strain. She planted her staff against the deck. The crystal at its tip flared, light meeting the bleeding resonance, forcing it back. Her voice rose, chanting in a language Kael couldn't understand, a song older than Meridian, older than the clans.

The bleeding slowed. The whispers dimmed.

But Kael saw the cost.

Blood welled at Liora's nose. Her hands shook violently, her skin pale as ash. The glow of the staff grew too bright, threatening to burn her from within.

Kael lunged forward, grabbing her arm. "Stop! You'll kill yourself!"

She didn't stop. Her eyes blazed. "If I stop, we all die."

Seris moved to her side, bracing her shoulders. Her voice was calm, iron steady. "Then we do this together. Take what strength you can from us."

The glow shifted. The capsule pulsed in rhythm with the staff now, the light forming threads that laced across the shard-heart's surface. Slowly, agonizingly, the cracks sealed. The whispers faded. The cavern stilled.

Then the glow shattered.

Light exploded outward, throwing Kael and Seris back against the walls. Liora screamed, her body arcing as though lightning tore through her veins. The staff's crystal cracked down the middle with a sound like breaking glass.

Kael scrambled up, his chest burning. He caught her as she collapsed, her body limp, her breath shallow.

"Liora!" His voice cracked. He shook her gently. "Stay with me!"

Her eyes fluttered open, barely. Her voice was a whisper. "The path… it's open. Deeper still. Don't… stop…"

Then she went limp in his arms.

The capsule hovered above the console, glowing steady now, a new line stretching deeper into the hollow. The way forward was clear.

But Kael didn't look at it. He held Liora, heart hammering, rage and fear twisting inside him. She had given everything to hold this place together. And she might not survive what came next.

Seris' hand gripped his shoulder, steady and grounding. "She bought us time. Don't waste it."

Kael swallowed hard, his jaw set. He laid Liora gently against the bulkhead, brushing a strand of hair from her face.

Then he stood, his eyes hard. "Fine. We keep going. But when this is over, someone's going to pay."

Chapter 26 – The Betrayer's Choice

The *Wraith's Fortune* clung to the edge of the hollow, hidden among the wrecks. Liora lay pale and unmoving in the crew berth, her staff cracked and dark beside her. Seris had taken first watch, standing at the viewport with her pistol on her hip, scanning the shadows.

Kael had been pacing the deck for hours. His nerves buzzed like live wires. Every time he looked at Liora's still form, his stomach twisted tighter. She had given everything to keep the shard-heart from bleeding them all into madness, and it had left her half-broken.

When the comm light flickered, Kael snapped his head up. A signal. Not from Seris' allies. Not from Meridian. From outside the hollow. A Riftborn warship.

Jorren.

Kael's chest went cold.

Seris glanced at him. "He's found you."

"Found *us*," Kael said bitterly. "But this isn't about you. It's about me."

Seris studied him for a long moment, then keyed the comm. The screen flared to life with Jorren's scarred face filling it, his implant eye glowing red against the gloom.

"Kael Veyra," Jorren growled. "Come out. Enough running."

Kael's throat tightened. He forced himself to speak. "You want me? You've got me. But the priestess stays here."

Jorren's lip curled. "You don't make the terms. You never did."

The line cut. Outside, Riftborn boarding skiffs detached from the warship and surged toward the *Fortune*.

Seris pulled her pistol. "We can hold them off long enough to jump deeper."

Kael shook his head. His voice was low, hard. "No. This is between me and him."

"Don't be a fool," Seris snapped.

Kael met her gaze. "I already was. Once. That's why we're here."

The Riftborn skiffs clamped onto the *Fortune's* hull with magnetic arms. Boots rang against the deck. Kael waited in the cargo hold, rifle slung across his chest, pistol at his hip. He didn't need to wait long.

The hatch blew. Smoke spilled in. Jorren stepped through, armor scarred, blade across his back. Behind him came half a dozen Riftborn warriors, but one sharp gesture sent them to the flanks. Jorren wanted this himself.

The two men stood facing each other across the hold.

Kael's voice was quiet. "It should have been me, not them."

Jorren's eye burned. "You don't get to speak their names."

Kael's fists clenched. "I'm not here to beg. I'm not here to justify. I'm here to finish what I left broken."

Jorren unslung his blade, the metal gleaming in the dim light. "Good. Then die standing, for once."

The fight was brutal, close, ugly. Jorren came at him with the weight of a warlord, every strike a hammer meant to break bone. Kael moved lighter, quicker, firing short bursts from his pistol, then ducking behind crates, striking when he could.

The cargo hold rang with gunfire and the crash of steel. Sparks flew as Jorren's blade split a crate in half. Kael rolled, firing point-blank. The bolt seared across Jorren's shoulder, but the man didn't falter. He swung again, and Kael barely caught the blade on his rifle, the impact sending pain lancing up his arms.

Jorren snarled. "You sold us to Meridian. For credits. For a ship."

Kael's jaw clenched. "For survival. I thought it would save us. I was wrong."

"You were a coward," Jorren spat. His blade slammed into the deck inches from Kael's chest as Kael rolled aside. "And cowards don't get second chances."

Kael staggered to his feet, blood running from a cut on his forehead. His chest heaved. "You're right. I don't deserve one. But she does."

He jerked his head toward the berth where Liora lay. "She's the only thing holding this Belt together. If you want to kill me, fine. Do it. But don't damn her with me."

Jorren froze for the barest heartbeat. His blade hovered. His implant eye whirred, adjusting focus.

Kael dropped his rifle. It clattered to the deck. He spread his arms wide, chest bare, throat open. "Here. Do it. End it. I won't run again."

The hold was silent but for the hum of the ship.

Jorren's chest rose and fell, scarred face twisted with rage. Then—slowly—he lowered the blade.

His voice was a rasp. "You don't deserve her loyalty. But she's not yours to damn."

Kael swallowed hard, relief and sorrow crashing through him. "Then fight with her. Fight with us. For once, fight for more than blood and fire."

Jorren's lip curled. His blade slammed back into its sheath. "I will fight—for my clan. For my dead. But if you falter again, Veyra, if you run once more, I will be the one to cut you down."

Kael nodded, his chest tight. "Fair enough."

Jorren turned, gestured to his warriors, and left as abruptly as he had come. The skiffs detached. The Riftborn warship pulled back into the shadows.

Kael stood alone in the hold, trembling, his breath ragged. His knees threatened to give, but he forced himself upright. He had faced the man he'd betrayed and lived. But it felt less like victory than a reprieve.

When he returned to the berth, Liora stirred faintly, whispering his name. He knelt beside her, brushing her hair from her face.

"It's all right," he murmured. "We're still here."

But he knew better. Nothing was all right. And what lay ahead would break them harder than the past ever had.

Chapter 27 — Engines of Heaven

The corridor spat them into a chamber so vast Kael's mind refused to measure it.

The *Wraith's Fortune* floated in silence, dwarfed by the scale. Crystal walls stretched outward into blackness, threaded with veins of pale fire. At the center of the void hung the Engine.

It was not a machine, not in any way Kael had words for. Vast structures spiraled around a core of light, fragments of shattered worlds drawn into orbit like asteroids. The light bled out in slow pulses, each one bending the void, warping the stars beyond. The hum of it filled Kael's skull until he could feel his own heartbeat syncing with it.

Seris whispered, "Engines of Heaven." Her voice was reverent, horrified. "I thought they were myth."

Kael gripped the console, knuckles white. "If that's a myth, I'd hate to see what counts as truth."

The capsule hovered above the console, brighter than Kael had ever seen it. Its lines reached toward the Engine, strands of light stitching together like threads longing to return home.

Liora stirred from the berth, weak but awake, her voice thin. "It's awake. The Shard remembers. All of them will, soon."

Kael turned to her sharply. "You shouldn't even be standing."

Her eyes glowed faintly in the Engine's light. "I have to. It's calling."

Before Kael could argue, alarms screamed.

Ships broke from the shadow of the chamber walls—Forge-State lancers, Riftborn skiffs, even Meridian cutters with stolen markings. And at their head, like a beast leading the hunt, *Ashfang*.

Drax had arrived.

The comm cracked alive, his voice rolling through every channel, iron and fire. "There it is. The core. The heart of the Belt. Today, the Forge becomes the law. Kill anyone who stands in the way. Bring me the priestess. Bring me the map."

Kael swore. "He followed us."

Seris' jaw was hard as steel. "Of course he did. We were the bait he needed."

Riftborn warships spilled into the chamber too, Jorren's *Bloodsong* at their head. The clans that had followed him roared into the fight, weapons blazing.

The chamber became chaos. Beams of molten light cut across the void. Skiffs darted, boarding hooks flashing. Explosions ripped against the crystal walls, the Engine's hum shifting with every impact, as though it were listening.

Kael threw the *Fortune* into a dive, weaving between wrecks drawn into the Engine's orbit. "This is suicide! We can't fight a Forge fleet here."

Liora's voice cut through the panic, fierce and sure despite her weakness. "We don't need to fight them. We need to wake the Engine."

Kael's blood went cold. "Wake it? Have you lost your mind? That thing will tear us apart!"

Her gaze was steady. "Or it will tear *them* apart."

Seris slammed a fresh mag into her pistol, bracing herself against the deck. "Then we better hope your instincts are sharper than theirs."

The capsule pulsed harder, the lines of light tightening into a single spear pointing toward the Engine's core.

Kael swallowed hard. "Of course. Straight into the mouth of hell."

He shoved the throttle forward. The *Fortune* roared into the light.

Drax stood on the *Ashfang's* command dais, gauntlet raised, his scarred face alight with hunger. He watched the *Fortune* dart into the Engine's glow and bared his teeth.

"Good," he growled. "Wake it for me."

He turned to his captains. "Field crew—bring the fragment online. We'll harness its heart before the Belt even knows what sings."

The mounted shard on the *Ashfang* flared. The field surged across the chamber, dragging ships off course, bending them into wrecks. Riftborn skiffs buckled under the weight, flames spilling into the void.

Still Kael pressed forward, the *Fortune* groaning, the capsule blazing with light.

Liora rose unsteadily, clutching her staff. She planted it against the deck, her eyes burning. "I can thread it. The Engine listens. It remembers. But I need—"

She staggered. Kael caught her, holding her steady. "What? What do you need?"

Her gaze met his, fierce despite her pallor. "You. Both of you. Anchor me. Or I won't come back."

Kael's heart pounded. "You want me to what—sing to a god-machine?"

Seris set her hand on Liora's shoulder without hesitation. "We hold. Do it."

Kael swore under his breath, then pressed his palm to Liora's other shoulder. "Fine. Just don't burn yourself out this time."

The staff flared. The capsule blazed.

And the Engine answered.

The light consumed the chamber. Kael felt himself ripped from the deck, from the ship, from his own skin. For an instant he saw everything—the Shards drifting in the Belt, the broken bridges of the old sky, the moment the Engines had torn the heavens apart. He felt the hunger of stone, the memory of fire, the grief of worlds that had been whole.

He gasped, choking, as he snapped back into himself. The *Fortune* bucked, the chamber shaking. The Engine pulsed harder now, its light spreading in great arcs across the void.

Drax's voice roared across comms, furious. "Control it! Now!"

But the Engine didn't listen.

It was awake.

And it was deciding what to do with those who had dared to touch it.

Chapter 28 – The Broken Sky

The chamber shook as the Engine woke.

The crystal walls rang like struck bells, their veins of light pulsing brighter, faster. Wrecks that had drifted for centuries snapped apart, metal bending into impossible shapes before disintegrating. The void itself seemed to warp, stars stretching and twisting through the light.

Kael gripped the *Fortune's* controls with white knuckles. Every warning light screamed red. Sparks spat from the console. The capsule on the dash spun slowly in the air, its glow so bright he could barely look at it.

"Whatever you're doing," he shouted over the alarms, "do it faster!"

Liora stood in the center of the cabin, staff braced against the deck. Her hair floated as though she stood in water, her eyes blazing with pale fire. The resonance pouring through her body bent the air, every breath a struggle. "It's not me—it's the Engine. It's... choosing."

Seris leaned against the viewport frame, braced against the vibration tearing through the hull. Her pistol was in her hand, though it was useless against what towered before them. Still, her gaze was steady, fierce. "Then tell it to choose quickly. We're about to be ash."

Outside, Forge-State lancers fired beams into the Riftborn lines. Explosions rocked the chamber, debris scattering. Jorren's *Bloodsong* surged at the *Ashfang*, ramming hard, boarding hooks flashing. Drax's voice boomed over the open comms, thick with fury and triumph.

"Hold the priestess! Seize the smuggler! The Engine is mine!"

The shard mounted on the *Ashfang* flared. Its field dragged Riftborn ships sideways, crumpling them like toys. Jorren roared defiance, his warship hammering back with fury.

Kael felt his stomach twist. He had hated Jorren, feared him, betrayed him. But now, seeing him throwing himself against Drax's monster, Kael felt something closer to respect.

"We're going to lose him," Kael muttered.

"No," Liora said. Her voice was distant, echoing as if layered with another tone. "Not if the Engine remembers."

The capsule pulsed. Threads of light lashed out from it, stitching into the Engine's surface. The pulses quickened, louder now, so loud Kael thought his skull would split.

And then—

They were not in the *Fortune*.

They were standing on a plain of glass under a shattered sky. Fragments hung above them, caught in frozen arcs, and in the distance rose towers that no one had built in Kael's lifetime. A voice spoke, not in words, but in memory.

The Engine showed them the day the heavens broke.

Kael saw bridges of light straining, engines shattering into brilliance. He saw worlds split, fire falling, oceans lifted into the void. And in the heart of it, he saw the Engines—not machines, not gods, but something in between. Vast structures alive with resonance, torn between creation and destruction.

He gasped as the vision burned through him, leaving him trembling. Seris' face was pale, her eyes wide with horrified understanding. Liora dropped to her knees, her staff clattering beside her, her breath ragged.

The voice pressed into them. A question.

Control... or destroy?

Kael staggered, clutching his head. "It's asking us to choose."

Seris' voice was hoarse but steady. "If Drax controls it, the Belt becomes his forge. If no one controls it, it tears itself apart—and us with it."

Liora lifted her head, eyes blazing faintly. "There's a third way. Not control. Not destruction. Balance. Let it remember without chains."

Kael barked a laugh, raw and desperate. "Balance? You've seen Drax's fleets. You've seen Meridian's rot. Balance doesn't survive men like that."

"Then we give it to the people who will fight for it," Liora said. Her gaze locked on his. "We give it to us."

The vision shattered. They were back in the cabin, alarms screaming. Outside, the battle raged. The *Ashfang* bore down on them, its shard-field burning like a second sun.

Drax appeared on their comm screen, face lit with fire, gauntlet raised. "You cannot stand against me. You cannot even stand against yourselves. Surrender the Engine, and I will let you live long enough to see what I make of your world."

Jorren's voice cut in, ragged with fury. "Kael! Priestess! Choose now, or we all burn!"

Kael's chest heaved. He looked at Liora, at Seris, at the capsule burning on the dash. He had spent his whole life running from choices. Now there was nowhere left to run.

His voice was low but steady. "We choose."

Liora planted her hands on the capsule. Seris covered one hand. Kael covered the other. Together, they poured their will into the light.

The Engine roared.

Light ripped through the chamber. The *Ashfang*'s shard shattered like glass, its field imploding. Forge-State ships spun out of control, crashing into crystal walls. Riftborn skiffs surged forward, striking hard.

Drax staggered as his command deck shook, his gauntlet sparking. He roared in fury. "This is not over! The Belt is mine!"

The Engine pulsed once more, sending a shockwave through the chamber. Riftborn, Forge-State, Meridian—all were hurled back, scattered.

When the light dimmed, only silence remained.

The *Wraith's Fortune* drifted in the heart of the chamber. The Engine had gone still. Not dead. Sleeping again. Waiting.

Liora slumped against the console, her eyes closing. Kael caught her before she fell. Seris stood over them, her face pale but resolute.

The Belt was broken. The war had begun. But for now, they had survived.

Chapter 29 – Fragments of Tomorrow

The *Wraith's Fortune* limped through the Drift, scars stitched across her hull. Panels sparked. Bulkheads groaned. The cabin reeked of burned circuits and smoke. But she was alive. So were they.

Kael sat at the console, hands loose on the controls. His whole body ached, and his head felt like it had been split open and stuffed with the Engine's hum. But he kept the *Fortune* steady, one eye always on the capsule.

It no longer blazed. Its light had dimmed to a faint pulse, as if sleeping. Kael hated the thought of it waking again.

Behind him, Liora lay in the berth, her breathing shallow but steadier than it had been. The cracks in her staff glowed faintly now, threads of resonance mending themselves like a wound trying to close. She had nearly given herself to the Engine, and Kael didn't know how much more she could give before it claimed her completely.

Seris stood at the viewport, arms folded, her cloak torn, her pistol holstered but close. She looked out into the Drift with the same calm as always, though Kael could see the weight in her shoulders. Meridian had branded her traitor. There was no path back for her. Only forward, with them.

Silence hung heavy until Seris broke it. "The Council will call this chaos. Drax will call it conquest. The Riftborn will call it betrayal. But whatever name they choose, the Belt will never be the same."

Kael let out a humorless laugh. "Good. The way it was didn't work anyway."

Seris' gaze flicked to him, sharp. "Do not fool yourself. They will come harder now. Forge-State fleets, Meridian assassins, Obsidian hunters. None of them will stop. You've set the fire. Now you'll have to live in the smoke."

Kael rubbed a hand over his face. "Not exactly the retirement I had in mind." He glanced back at Liora, softer. "But I'm not running. Not anymore."

The capsule pulsed faintly, as if it had heard him.

Elsewhere, across the Belt, fragments shifted.

On Varak, Drax stood before the broken remains of the *Ashfang's* shard, its field shattered, its fragments cold. His gauntlet smoked, but his eyes burned brighter than ever. He turned to his captains, voice a growl. "The Engine woke for them. That means it can wake for us. Build me more. Bigger. Stronger. Until the sky itself bows."

In Meridian Prime, Councilor Venn stood on the balcony of the glass chamber, the city glittering beneath him. He held Seris' name scrawled across a warrant and smiled thinly. "Let her run. Let her burn. Every traitor leaves a trail. And every trail leads to power."

In the shadows of a forgotten wreck, the Assassin sat perfectly still. Its mask tilted toward the dark, listening. The Engine's hum still echoed faintly through the void. The Order's voice filled the silence. *Silence failed. Silence must be reforged.* The Assassin's blade slid free with a soft hiss. It would not fail again.

And in the Riftborn halls, Jorren stood before his clan, blood on his armor, his voice like fire. "We stood against the Forge and lived. The priestess may carry the Shards' song, but it was our blades that cut the path. Remember that. When the Belt chooses sides, it will be Riftborn steel that decides the ending."

Back aboard the *Fortune*, Kael checked their course. The capsule's light pulsed once, twice, harder than before, casting its glow across his scarred hands. It wasn't finished. Not by half.

He looked at Seris, then at Liora's resting form. His throat tightened. "We should turn back."

Seris' voice was calm, final. "There is no back. Only forward."

Kael closed his eyes. For once, he didn't argue.

The *Fortune* slipped into the dark, the capsule's glow burning like a beacon.

The Belt had broken once.

Now it was breaking again.

And this time, they were at the center of it.

About the Author

Alan Hawky is a science fiction writer fascinated by broken worlds, flawed heroes, and the fire that binds people together. The Shattered Orbits is the first book of the Rift Cycle, his epic debut space opera series.

Coming Soon
Book Two of the Rift Cycle

The Shards are stirring. The Engines of Heaven have only begun to wake. Kael, Liora, and Seris have survived the first storm—but the Drift hides darker paths still to come. The fire has only just begun.

Printed in Dunstable, United Kingdom